REVENGE
JASON STEED

MARK A. COOPER

sourcebooks
jabberwocky

Published by Sourcebooks Jabberwocky, an imprint of Sourcebooks, Inc.
P.O. Box 4410, Naperville, Illinois 60567-4410
(630) 961-3900
Fax: (630) 961-2168
www.jabberwockykids.com

Library of Congress Cataloging-in-Publication data is on file with the publisher.

Source of Production: Bang Printing, Brainerd, Minnesota, USA
Date of Production: February 2012
Run Number: 16843

Printed and bound in the United States of America.
BG 10 9 8 7 6 5 4 3 2 1

I dedicate this book to my wonderful wife, Sandra.
Thank you for being my partner and my best friend
and for the way you make me laugh.

CHAPTER 1

THE YAMAHA RD 250 motorcycle circled at the end of Tower Hill Terrace. It was just going to be bad luck for the rider that one of the people in the line was eleven-year-old Jason Steed.

Princess Catherine stood in line with Jason; she wore a knitted red hat and glasses with plain lenses so the hundreds of tourists that surrounded them at the Tower of London would not recognize her.

Slowly the long line moved forward. Some of the excited tourists took photographs of the historic buildings. A Yeoman Warder walked passed. Many in the line quickly took a picture of him dressed in a smart purple and red uniform. He carried a large spear-shaped mace with a polished, solid silver point.

"This line's hardly moving. It will take at least another twenty minutes to get in at this rate," Catherine complained, leaning heavily on Jason.

"Well, this is what *normal* people do, but if you wanna take off your glasses and hat and let everyone see who you are and walk to the front, go ahead," Jason said, grinning.

The motorcyclist slowly made his way up Tower Hill Terrace. In a low gear with high revs, the rider removed his left hand from the handlebars, pulled close to the long line of waiting tourists, and grabbed the straps of two purses. He accelerated and pulled the purses free from the startled owners; the motorcycle's front wheel momentarily left the ground as he gained speed. Screams and shouts caught the attention of others as he roared up the narrow street, almost knocking into some of the tourists, and the line snaked out of his way.

Jason had seen it and was already moving in the direction of the Yeoman Warder, who was backing away to allow a gap for the speeding motorcycle. In a single move, Jason grabbed the mace with one hand, pushed the Yeoman back out of the way with the other, and jumped into the path of the motorcycle. The rider didn't slow or try to alter course; he was sure this foolish boy would move out of his way. At the last second, Jason jumped clear, but as he did, he thrust the spear into the front wheel. A loud crack echoed across the street like gunfire as the silver tip of the mace jammed between the front wheel spokes and the frame.

The front wheel instantly locked up, and the motorcycle catapulted the rider over the handlebars and sent him sprawling across the cobblestone street. The crowd screamed and gasped as the motorcycle whooshed into flames. The dazed rider got to his feet and started to run. Jason took off and tackled him, bringing him down to the ground for a second time.

The rider struck out at Jason and caught the side of his face. He kicked Jason and managed to get to his feet again. Jason paused—the punch on the side of his face had really hurt. The rider shouted obscenities and spat at Jason. That was enough to tip Jason over the edge; he leapt onto one leg and threw a mae geri kick. The powerful kick ripped off the rider's helmet, causing the chin strap to cut deep into his neck before the buckle broke. Jason followed with a roundhouse kick directly to the man's face.

The injured rider collapsed on the cobblestones, oozing blood from his nose and neck wound. Two police officers on nearby traffic duty ran to the scene. The rider was escorted away in handcuffs, swearing at Jason all the while.

Jason picked up the ladies' purses and returned them; his crimson face glowed with embarrassment as the crowd applauded him. The Yeoman took Jason and Catherine to the front of the line and allowed them into the tower without having to pay.

"Wow, Jase, that was amazing," she remarked as she proudly held his hand. "You moved so fast."

"I did it to stop your complaining. See, we don't have to wait in line now."

Catherine loved going out alone with Jason. She could forget about being a princess and all the pressure associated with it. Today, she was just a young, pretty girl out with her boyfriend on a visit to the Tower of London. They later settled down on a bench and shared a bag of chips, looking out over the River Thames.

Any onlooker watching this little, blond-haired boy sitting and laughing on a bench with a young girl would never have guessed that in a few weeks, he would be the most wanted person in Europe.

CHAPTER 2

T HE YOUNG OFFENDERS UNIT housed some of London's toughest teenage criminals; among them was Andrew Cho, the son of the notorious Triad leader, Lin Cho. He would be Jason's cell mate.

"Battersea Borstal for Boys," the sign read. A young offenders unit for boys aged eleven to sixteen—this was to be Jason's home for the next four weeks.

"Sorry, son, you have to put these on." He smiled as he placed handcuffs tightly on Jason's wrists. "I did you a favor—you should have had them on while traveling, but you being so small, well, I didn't think you could do me any harm." Little did he know *who* this boy was or what he was capable of.

Jason's leg painfully came back to life as he straightened it. He had been kneeling so he could see out the window. He limped out the back of the van, feeling his wrist where he would normally wear his watch.

As Jason looked at his surroundings, the wind chased through his blond hair and the spray of rain danced in his eyes. He followed the driver through the large dark door that led to a courtyard with cloisters on two sides and two bell towers rising up from the others. They went through another arch door. Inside, it smelled of disinfectant. A tall, balding prison guard removed Jason's handcuffs and gestured for Jason to follow him down a corridor. Sounds of boys shouting, laughing, and cursing could be heard.

"Get undressed and take a shower, and don't be all day, lad."

He was given a plastic bag for his clothes, and he was pleasantly surprised to find the shower's water warm. The guard lit a cigarette and watched him.

"What are those marks on your stomach and leg? Have you been burned?" he asked, looking at Jason.

"Yes, sir, but it's nearly healed now," he replied quietly.

The truth was that he had just come out of plastic surgery to have two bullet wounds surgically covered, but he knew he was going to be forced to tell a lot more lies before the next four weeks were over.

"Okay, that's enough. I ain't got all blooming night." He grunted as he threw a towel. "Follow me." Jason wrapped the towel around his waist. He felt nervous. The shouts were getting louder and the smells stronger, and it seemed colder.

What a difference a day makes. He smiled to himself.

Only yesterday, he had passed his pilot's license. At eleven, he was the youngest person in Britain ever to achieve this. Unlike a driver's license, a pilot's license had no age minimum. The flying lessons were a gift from his father. It had been easy for Jason after he had spent so many hours in flight simulators. The practical lessons themselves had been a walk in the park. The technical side he had found hard, but he hadn't expected it to be easy.

But that was yesterday. Today he was working undercover for Scotland Yard Undercover Intelligence. His father, Lieutenant Raymond Steed, was away on the navy aircraft carrier HMS *Ark*

Royal and knew nothing of this. His last word was that Jason should have nothing to do with it, as he was too young and had already done enough for his country. However, the head of SYUI, George Young, could be very persuasive, and Jason's eagerness to work for SYUI got the better of him.

SYUI had heard that a criminal organization known as the Triads were raising millions of pounds across Britain. The tip-off had led them to believe that Lin Cho had masterminded the whole dirty operation. He was the Triad leader in London. The Triads in Britain owned bars, managed illegal gambling halls, sold drugs, and ran a protection racket. They supposedly offered shop owners protection from robberies. In practice, they charged a fortune, and if you refused to pay, your shop would get robbed and the store owner beaten or worse. Cho's son, Andrew, was serving time in juvie. It was Jason's job to get close to Andrew to find out how they were raising so much money and what it was for. SYUI knew most of it was being transferred back to China, but they didn't know what the Triads were planning.

Jason was given three pairs of socks, underwear, and three gray T-shirts that were originally white but had turned gray after they had been washed over and over with the gray socks and overalls. He was also given a gray, shapeless overall. He got dressed, rolling up the pant legs that were much too long for him. Fortunately, his pair of black tennis shoes fit.

"Right, lad, off to see the governor. Come on, it's late, and he'll be wanting to go home."

"Maybe I can go home too, sir," Jason said, forcing a smile.

"You are too small to be cocky, lad. If you want to survive in here, you will do yourself a favor and keep your trap shut."

"Yes, sir," he quietly replied with his head bowed.

He followed the guard and rolled his sleeves up so his hands were free. They stopped outside a large oak door with a brass plate that read "Governor Brown." The guard knocked and waited until he heard a "Come."

"This is another new one. Let me introduce Mr. Jason Steed, sir," the guard said, walking in and reading from a brown file. "Repeat shoplifter, sir. Four weeks."

Jason actually felt guilty, even though he was innocent. If George was right, then the governor was the only man inside juvie who knew Jason was working undercover.

"Okay, Johnson, leave us for a while. I want to tell him how I want him to behave and explain the rules," Brown replied. "Sit down, Steed. Take a cookie." He gestured for Jason to sit down and took the lid off a metal tin that was full of chocolate chip cookies.

Then Governor Brown started to laugh. His pale, strangely featureless face turned red as he laughed. He pushed his fingers through his curly gray hair. Jason, not sure what the problem was, took a cookie.

"Sorry, there must be a mistake. I was told that a Jason Steed was coming here and working undercover for SYUI."

"That's right, sir," Jason said with a mouthful of the cookie.

"But you're…you're what? Eleven? Twelve? What can a little, blond-haired, blue-eyed boy like you possibly do? How can you look after yourself? No, it's out of the question. I can't put you in a cell with Andrew Cho. You will be dead by morning. We have an arrangement. He keeps out of trouble and doesn't hurt the other inmates, and in return, he has a cell to himself. He will kick you from here to kingdom come." He laughed again, which annoyed Jason.

"I'm a black belt in judo, black belt in jujitsu and shotokan, and hold a third dan black belt in tae kwon do. SYUI went to a lot of trouble to get me to go along with this. My dad will go crazy when he finds out. I'd much rather be in my own home. *This* is not a vacation for me."

Brown examined Jason, clearly impressed.

"If you're sure you can take care of yourself. Well, huh…no one will suspect you, that's for sure." He laughed. "But…no special treatments. Once you leave my office, you are on your own. I will treat you like everyone else. If you get hurt, don't come crying to me." Brown spat out his words and sprayed saliva over the cookies. Jason made a mental note not to eat any more.

"I know. I've a job to do, sir." Jason looked at him through the blond bangs that hung over his eyes.

He was taken to the cell blocks. The other inmates were playing cards and table tennis and arm wrestling. He followed the guard up a metal stairway as he carried his bedding.

"Here we are. Home sweet home. Although I have no idea why the gov has put you in with Andrew Cho. He is not going to like it one bit. Good luck," the guard said, ushering Jason into the cell.

Jason looked around the cell. The top bunk was made up; the

bottom bunk had just a thin, stained mattress, with underwear and socks placed out neatly. It had a toilet in the corner and a small stainless steel sink. A single toothbrush was lying on top of the sink. He removed the clothing and placed it on the top bunk and made up his bed. He had been in here only a short while and he already hated it.

"What the—" a spot-faced, red-haired boy in the doorway started. It was an older boy named Russell Watson. This was Watson's second time in juvie; he had been sentenced to three months, the same as Andrew, for stealing cars. Andrew had been sentenced for assaulting a police officer after he had been caught kicking the owner of a store half to death.

"Hello," Jason said, not making eye contact.

"You can't touch Cho's stuff. What on Earth are you doing in there?"

"Home sweet home." Jason grinned.

"Are you trying to be funny, shrimp?"

"No."

"You're dead, shrimp. Cho will kick your 'ed in. He has a cell to himself."

Watson walked off, talking to himself. Jason lay back on his bunk. He was tired; he hadn't slept much the night before, worrying about being held in juvie. He closed his eyes for what seemed like only minutes before he was woken up.

"See, I told you. You got a little shrimp in your cell, and he's moved yer clothes," Watson said loudly, pointing down at Jason. Jason opened his eyes and sat up.

"You need to thank God you are so small. Get your things

and get out of my cell. I will be back in five minutes, and *you* had better just be a bad memory!" Andrew shouted.

Andrew was Chinese but spoke with an English accent. Jason thought he was tall for a fifteen-year-old. He had short dark hair and chocolate-brown eyes with acne on his face. Andrew and Watson walked off. Jason said nothing.

I guess I had better get to work and show them I can't be messed with. He followed them back down the metal stairway to the large open hall, trying to think of way to start a fight.

CHAPTER 3

MANY OF THE BOYS in the hall were chatting and laughing in groups. They all wore the same black tennis shoes and gray overalls. Some sat around tables and played cards. A couple played table tennis while others watched. Jason noticed Andrew and Watson with a group of similarly aged boys. They all wore their collars popped and sleeves rolled up. Watson was bullying a smaller boy. He twisted the boys nipples through his clothing, and the boy cried out in obvious pain, pleading for mercy. He was forced to call Watson all sorts of grand names before Watson finally let him go after a final twist. The boy fell to the ground amid laughter and wiped the tears from his cheeks.

Jason stared at Watson. He hated bullies—this was enough to give him the excuse he needed. After a few minutes, Watson noticed and looked at Jason and then looked away. Jason kept the stare, and after a moment, Watson noticed he was still being glared at.

"What's 'e looking at? Hey, shrimp! What you looking at?" Watson shouted to Jason. Jason shook his head from side to side and gave a dirty, disgusted look.

"He's asking for it," Watson said and started to stride toward Jason. Andrew and the other boys in the group watched.

"So what you looking at shrimp?" he sternly asked again.

"Sorry, was I staring? But I guess you must get that a lot,

being that you're so ugly. I bet when you were born, the doctor took one look at you and then slapped your mama." Jason smiled broadly and slowly raised himself onto his toes.

Watson's face went bright red, his eyes popping out of his skinny face; he cursed at Jason and threw a punch. Jason ducked and spun around on his left leg and carried out a full roundhouse kick that made contact under Watson's chin. Watson's head jerked back. His teeth clacked together, and he fell on his back. He must have bitten his tongue because blood started to pour from his mouth. Andrew walked forward. Watson was quick to get to his feet and ran at Jason, swinging wildly with his fists. Jason stood firm and blocked each blow with his arms. He then counter-punched Watson, catching him square on the nose.

Again, Watson cursed at Jason, blood running from his nose. He picked up a chair and swung it in Jason's direction. Jason ducked, dove to the floor on his hands, and spun his legs around, sweeping Watson's feet. Watson's legs were thrown into the air, and he fell heavily on his back. Jason pounced on his prey, landing with his knee in Watson's chest. He threw four incredibly fast punches to Watson's face and climbed off him.

"Hmm, some improvement to your face now," Jason joked. A roar of laughter went up from the other boys who started to gather around them. They went quiet and moved back when Andrew slowly approached.

"Shrimp, you're pretty good. What form of karate do you practice?" he asked with arms folded.

"The name is Steed. Jason Steed. If we're to be roommates, *you* need to know that. I practice tae kwon do."

Andrew nodded and studied Jason while in deep thought. He ruled juvie—no one had dared speak to him like this before. He watched Jason walk back up the metal stairway and then focused his attention on Watson.

"You are pathetic. You let a little kid do that to you. You're an embarrassment. I can't be seen going around with you. Find yourself some new friends," Andrew shouted at Watson, who was trying to get up from the floor with one hand while the other hand held his bloody nose.

Andrew waited until it was bedtime before he returned to his cell.

"You're still here then, shrimp? I thought I told you to get out. Just because you kick the stuffing out of Watson, you think you can ignore me?" Andrew said in the doorway of the cell.

Jason ignored him. He sat on the bottom bunk, picking his feet. Andrew slowly entered and stood in a fighting stance, glaring at Jason.

"I told you my name, Andrew. It's Jason, not shrimp. You're Chinese. Do you want me to call you 'takeaway'?"

Andrew glared and raised his top lip. He was about to attack Jason when the cell door slammed and Jason heard two bolts being drawn across.

"Night, lads. Pleasant dreams. Good luck, blondie," said the prison guard. Jason could hear the guard's footsteps fade into the distance. Suddenly, everything was silent. He was alone with Andrew.

Andrew looked at Jason. He was bemused by him. This little pretty boy did not seem to have a care in the world and was not threatened by him.

"I don't get it. You not only move into my cell and kick the stuffing out of Watson, but now you call me 'takeaway.' Do you have a death wish? Have you any idea who I am?"

Jason stood up. He looked up at Andrew and forced a smile. "I've no idea why they put me in with an older boy or who you are, and I don't really care. Don't blame me for being put into your stinking cell. I'm not a shrimp. I'm just younger than you. We can either fight it out or we just make the most of it." Jason held out his hand.

Andrew ignored it and walked over to use the toilet, cursing under his breath. He didn't speak. They got undressed and climbed into their bunks. Jason was shaking; he was still nervous. George told him that Andrew and his father were ruthless. If Andrew wanted to strangle him in the night, he was big enough and Jason would have a tough job fighting him off. It was another three hours before he finally got to sleep.

The next few days, Andrew said nothing to Jason. He ignored him, and he complained to the governor about having to share a cell. He was given the excuse that the juvenile center was short of space. Governor Brown told Andrew that he chose Jason because he was small and quiet and should not get in Andrew's way. Andrew, although clearly unhappy, swallowed the story whole.

George Young held a meeting at the offices of SYUI with MI5, MI6, and Metropolitan police commissioner John Lock. His direct superior, Simon Caldwell, was also there. Caldwell was George's age and slim with short gray hair. He was, as usual, wearing an expensive-looking Italian suit and gold watch. They sat around the large, open office in the dark, looking at images on a projector screen. George's voice clipped with authority despite his heavy London East End accent. He dropped in rhyming slang words at every sentence—something that amused the onlookers. It was sometimes difficult for them to decipher George's meaning. In East London, slang speakers replaced words or phrases with other words that rhymed. For example, bread rhymes with head. So the phrase "loaf of bread" means head. East Enders will say "use your loaf" instead of "use your head."

George pointed at a large screen with an unlit cigarette. "This is Lin Cho, an evil sod and head of the London Triads. He's bloody ruthless and has a reputation for the most violent crimes. Many people inside his own organization fear him."

He flicked the switch to show another image: a very large Asian man dressed in a suit. He looked like a sumo wrestler with short, cropped hair, and his neck seemed to be all part of his wide shoulders. "This is Kotang, Cho's bodyguard and driver. He is Japanese and can crush a feller in his bare arms. I wouldn't want to meet up with this bloke on a dark night."

He showed an image of a Chinese woman in a blond wig. She was wearing knee-length black leather boots, tight leopard-skin pants, and a black leather jacket.

"This is Boudica. She's the 'Mr. Big'—head of the entire

Triad organization in the United Kingdom. In my view, the most dangerous person in the world. Lin Cho is her number two in the UK.

"The new Chinese police commissioner, Lin Tse-Hsu, is tracking her down and trying to stop her corruption back in China. She is sending huge amounts of money back to China from the UK. And I mean huge amounts—in the millions. Intel has it that she is unhappy with the Mao government and the new laws of one baby per family. The rumor is that she gave birth to two children and that one was taken and killed by government officials. Unfortunately, the child she was left with later died of pneumonia. She completely snapped. Three Chinese maternity wards were ripped apart by explosives, killing hundreds."

"Yes, I remember hearing about that," John Lock sighed.

"They never found the culprit, but some Chinese detectives think it was her work, and she fled when they got close."

He showed another image. It was of a young Asian teenager.

"This is Andrew, Lin Cho's only son and a right little terror. He is currently serving time in juvenile detention. We have a man on the inside who is sharing a cell and befriending him. He will get the information about what the Triads are up to out of Andrew Cho."

"So this inside man, he must be the same age—what? Sixteen? Seventeen?" Lock asked with his eyebrows raised.

"He's not quite that age, but he's the best we have. He holds the Victoria Cross and Queen's Award for Bravery. He's a black belt in more karate disciplines than I can name and is also the youngest qualified pilot in Britain. He is also fluent in a variety of languages."

"Good God, man. You mean that *boy*—what's his name?—um…Jason Steed? He's barley twelve and just got out of the hospital," John snorted.

"He's the best there is, mate. Plus, no one will suspect him. He'll get the information we need. I stake my reputation on it," George affirmed before he turned off the projector.

"I hope you're right, George. We have a lot riding on this," Caldwell said.

George was confident in Jason. He could think of no one else he would trust to go undercover…and survive.

CHAPTER 4

THE FOURTH DAY, JASON had still not managed to get Andrew to speak to him. Jason was given mopping duty, and he spent three hours a day mopping corridors and three hours in school.

Every other day, depending on what block they were on, the boys had to shower. Today in Block B, where Jason and Andrew shared a cell, was shower day. As they walked down to the shower block with a towel around their waists, Jason noticed some of the other boys talking and looking back at him. At first he ignored it, but as they approached the shower blocks, it became more obvious to him that something was going to happen.

The shower contained twelve showerheads fixed to a wall, another wall keeping back the water. This also hid users from the view of any passing guards—not that they had ever come into the shower block. It was like a thinly tiled hallway with one entry. The rest of the block was filled with sinks and toilets. Jason went to the far end and started to take a shower. He wanted to keep his back to the end wall so he could see what was going to happen. He knew it was a bad idea to position himself in a dead end, but he was confident in his ability to protect himself.

Andrew entered and took a shower in the center. As Andrew washed his hair, he closed his eyes. The rest of the boys all left the shower area, which left just Jason and Andrew showering. Jason turned the shower to cold; he wanted to keep his body as awake as he could.

Three boys entered the shower; they had their towels in their hands. At the ends, the towels were tied into a pouch with small rocks inside. It made a brutal weapon when swung with force. Watson had one. The other two boys Jason had seen around but could not name them. Another two boys stood at the entrance of the shower. As they twisted the towels, Jason climbed to the balls of his feet. He thought he was going to be attacked by the boys and Andrew, but as they approached, he noticed they were not watching him. Then one put his finger up to his lips and gestured for Jason to remain silent.

It's not me. It's Andrew they're after, Jason thought to himself.

As they approached, Watson raised his towel and swung it at Andrew, catching him by surprise in the face. He fell back heavily against the tiled wall. The other two also swung at him, but he soon jumped to his feet to defend himself. He was fast and threw out a kick, catching one of the boys in the throat and knocking him to the shower floor. Two other boys entered and jumped Andrew. He was soon overpowered. Two held him with his arms behind his back. Watson approached and swung his towel at Andrew and caught him in his groin. Andrew screamed in pain, and his legs buckled. He was being held up by the arms and blood trickled from his mouth.

"What was it you called me, Cho? Pathetic embarrassment? Who's pathetic now?" Watson shouted. He spat in Andrew's face. "So you think you're 'Mr. Big'? You aren't so big now, are ya?" He lifted his weighted towel once more to take a swing.

"Leave him alone," Jason ordered, walking toward them.

"Look, it's Cho's pretty blond boyfriend. I have something else in mind for you, shrimp," Watson snarled, winking.

Jason ran and jumped. He kicked out at Watson, the heel of his right foot connecting with Watson's nose. Jason ducked as a weighted towel was swung at his head. Andrew's captors released Andrew and turned to fight Jason. One by one, Jason kicked out, balancing on his left leg and switching to his right. He blocked all counterpunches and fought four of the boys single-handed. Blood sprayed a wall as Jason's fist connected with another boy's nose. As he tried to kick out at one boy, Jason's foot slipped on the wet floor. He lost his balance and fell on his back.

Watson had recovered and towered over him about to bring down a heavy, wet towel full of rocks. Jason braced for the hit, raising his arms to protect his face, but before it happened, Watson screamed out in pain and fell to the wet floor holding his leg. Jason jumped to his feet.

What happened to Watson?

Then he saw Andrew throwing a final kick to the face of the last boy standing. He had kicked Watson's leg from behind and shattered the boy's knee. The five young boys lay on the floor, groaning, blood running from their noses and mouths. Watson was in tears, screaming in pain, holding his knee.

Back in the cell, Jason and Andrew got dressed. Andrew gingerly touched his still-bleeding lip.

"It's okay. You don't have to thank me." Jason grinned.

"I didn't ask for your help. I can look after myself," Andrew grunted.

"Oh, yeah, how much longer could you have taken being hit with those weighted towels?"

"I didn't *need* your help…but thanks. How did you learn to fight like that?"

"I've been at a load of foster homes, and I always make sure I have my foster parents take me to a local karate school. I'm just good at it."

"I can't put my finger on it, but something's not right about you." Andrew sighed and looked deep into Jason's blue eyes.

There is no way my cover is blown. Shrug it off, Jason thought to himself.

"Look at you. Good looking, pretty blue eyes, blond hair, and you speak posh. You never swear, and you're always deep in thought. How did *you* learn to fight like that? I'm a black belt—what are you?"

"Black belt. Sorry if I speak posh. I was brought up by a posh family. Is that a crime?"

Jason failed to mention he was a third dan black belt as well as Hong Kong's under-sixteen karate champion. Jason's defeated opponent, Jet Chan, later went on to win the under-sixteen world championship in Jason's absence.

Two hours later, Jason and Andrew were ordered to see the governor.

"I have five boys who reported to the hospital ward. One has a shattered knee. Others have broken noses and cracked ribs. A little bird tells me you two had something to do with it. What happened?" Governor Brown screamed.

Jason shrugged his shoulders.

"The little bird is wrong. I've been playing cards with my cell mate, Jason," Andrew replied.

Governor Brown noticed Jason's knuckles. His soft skin had broken open, and there was dried blood on his fingers.

"Then how did you do that to your knuckles, Steed? And what happened to your lip, Cho?"

Jason didn't know what to say. *Is he going to blow my cover?* Andrew came to his rescue.

"I said we were playing cards. We played snap, and it got a little rough. He has hands like a baby. And as for my lip, well, I caught my face on the bunk. I'm not used to having to step around a little shrimp all the time."

"I don't buy that. I will be watching you two. Get out of my sight," Brown snapped.

Jason, pleased with Andrew's remarks, couldn't help smirking.

"Funny, is it, Steed? We will see just how funny it is when you feel the cane!" Governor Brown shouted. He pulled a cane out of his desk drawer. "Hold out your hand."

Jason fearlessly held out his hand.

"You can go, Cho." The guard led Andrew away. Jason expected the governor wanted to talk to him in private.

Whack!

Jason got the shock of his life. When Andrew left, Brown brought the cane down hard on his hand.

"What the—" Jason shouted and held back from cursing at the governor. "You hit me for real," Jason protested, shocked.

"Hold out your hand again. I have not finished."

"Are you stupid?" he cursed. "Have you forgotten why I'm

here? You don't have to really cane me. Andrew's gone. He won't know you didn't really hit me."

"Look at your hand, Steed."

Jason looked at the palm of his hand. He had a red line across it from the cane. It was throbbing and stinging like a bad burn.

"If you go back to your cell without some red marks on your hand, your cover could be blown. I told you no special treatment. Now hold out your hand. You need at least two marks on your hand."

This undercover work stinks.

CHAPTER 5

JASON STOOD PATIENTLY WITH another thirty or so boys. It was Saturday, so Jason had survived six days. Today, some of the inmates were receiving visitors.

"Okay, you know the rules. No exchanging items. No contact with another inmate's visitors. Go to the table with your visitor and sit," a guard told the boys.

As they made their way into the large hall, Jason's eyes darted around for his best friend, Scott Turner. No one would have any reason to suspect a boy Jason's age coming to visit. Jason could give him an update, and Scott would report back to SYUI.

So that must be Lin Cho, the head Triad, Jason said to himself as he watched Andrew hug an older man and then kiss the woman next to him. Mr. Cho was dressed in black. He was bald, and Jason thought he looked too old to have a fifteen-year-old son. Jason had walked between the tables to the end of the large hall but could not see Scott.

Maybe he's not coming.

He slowly walked back, disappointed. Every table had a family smiling and sharing gossip. Then he noticed a table on the end. One person sat there wearing a hat, a long raincoat with the collar pulled up, and sunglasses. It was Scott.

"What on Earth are you wearing?" Jason gasped when he recognized him.

"Shhh. Keep your voice down," Scott whispered.

"Have you any idea what you look like?" Jason said, pulling the sunglasses off his friend and laughing.

"Jason…give them back. I'm undercover, remember?" he hissed back.

Jason roared with laughter. Many of the visitors and inmates around looked up to see who was laughing so loud. Andrew looked across and smiled.

"Stop it, you dodo. You'll give me away," objected Scott.

"Scott, I love you, mate. You always make me laugh. You don't have to dress up like a spy. Your cover is that you are just a regular boy my age." He continued to laugh.

"Yes…I know. I was just trying to cheer you up and it worked," Scott said looking hurt and removing his hat. He then took Jason's hands and looked at his cut and bruised knuckles.

"I see you've been busy. Does Cho trust you yet?"

"Yeah, I had to make an entrance. Andrew and I get on okay. We actually have a lot in common. He's quite good at karate and knows tons about Bruce Lee films."

"Oh, so it's Andrew now. Remember why he's here."

"I know. This place is horrible. The food sucks. The bed sucks. The whole place smells, and every other word the boys use is a curse word."

"Well, they're not the type to go to our school, are they? Can you imagine 'Taffy' Griffiths at St. Joseph dealing with these boys?"

"No, he'd have a heart attack. How is school anyway? Anyone miss me?"

"No, just me. Catherine called me and said to say hi. Mum

and Dad said hello. Actually, some of the teachers and others in our class have started to call you the 'wonder child.'"

"Really?" Jason said, smiling, pleased with his new nickname.

"Yeah, they 'wonder' if you're ever going to learn anything."

"Hey, that's not funny. I know I'm missing school, but I'll be back soon. How are your parents?"

"Fine. Well, actually, Mum has been on my case. One minute, I'm wrong for not eating breakfast, and now I'm wrong for eating too many Coco-Bites. Yeah, I'll admit I can finish a whole box in two days, but it's so good! Maybe I'm going through a growth spurt. Do I look taller?"

"A whole box in two days? You'll *look* like a Coco-Bite at that rate," Jason laughed.

After an hour, a buzzer sounded and the visitors started to get up and go. Scott stood up to leave, and Jason grabbed his hand. Jason's eyes welled up as he tried to smile. Scott bent down and hugged him.

"I'll see you next week, mate. Stay safe." It was hurtful for Scott to see his friend getting upset. He wondered if his father had been right when he had suggested Jason was too young to cope with it emotionally.

"Who's your friend? A cousin?" Andrew asked Jason as he climbed onto his bunk and kicked off his shoes. Jason didn't want to answer. Scott was his best friend—everything that Andrew was not. Jason now realized how much he missed being home with Mrs. Beeton, his school, Scott making him laugh—and, of course, he missed Princess Catherine.

"He's just a good friend."

26

"He speaks posh like you. Do you go to the same school?"

"We have. Was that your parents?" Jason asked, trying to change the subject.

"Yeah, my parents were born in China, but I was born here."

"What does your father do?" Jason asked, not knowing if it was too early to start asking questions.

"I don't know if I can say."

"Be like that. I thought we were friends. But if it's a state secret—"

"No, we *are* friends. Let's just say he's works in gray areas."

"So he's a thief? Nothing wrong with that. Although, look at us. We all get caught in the end."

Andrew jumped down from his bunk and glared at Jason. "He's not a thief. You have no idea, do you?" Andrew snapped. "He is head of the Triads in London. About two hundred people work for him."

"Triads. That's what? Chinese mafia?" Jason muttered, trying to act dumb.

Andrew sat next to Jason on his bunk and explained how the Triads worked. His father was number one in the whole of London. There was also a group in Manchester and Glasgow. The head of all of them was Boudica.

"Bodia whata?" Jason asked with a grin.

"It doesn't matter. Never repeat her name."

The next few days went by with no problems. Jason and Andrew started to spar and practice karate together, and Andrew was constantly surprised by Jason's speed and the different moves he could perform. One afternoon while they were walking back to their cell, Watson stood in front of them on the walkway. As they approached, he tried to move away.

"I've not forgotten you, Watson. I hope you've made a will," Andrew hissed.

Watson retreated, saying nothing.

"I'm going to kill him," Andrew told Jason as they entered the cell. Jason ignored the remark. Later, as they undressed and climbed into their bunks and the guards shouted, "Lights out," Andrew repeated it: "Tomorrow, he will die."

"What will you do? Give him another kicking and break his other leg?"

"I'm going to kill him. No one does that to a Cho and lives."

"Come on, Andrew. You can't really kill him," Jason said, concerned.

"This time tomorrow, he will be a corpse."

Jason couldn't sleep. He wondered if he should warn Watson—maybe speak to Governor Brown and get Watson moved, although that could blow his cover. He hated it here. He hated the food and the guards that looked down on him and treated him like a criminal. He did not want this all to be for nothing. He had to continue with the mission and get the information for SYUI.

Jason woke early in the morning. He was doing push-ups on the floor of the cell when Andrew finally woke. Andrew watched him.

"Andrew, you're not going to really kill him, are you?" Jason puffed.

"Why, have you gone soft? Do you have any idea what Watson had in store for you when they attacked us in the bathroom?"

"No, I thought maybe a good kicking."

"Jason, you're so naïve. Some younger boys get burned in here. An older boy will brand a younger boy with his initials just like cattle. *That's* what he had in store for *you*."

Jason went quiet; he was shocked by Andrew's remark. What had he got himself in for? What sort of place had George sent him to? The sooner this was over, the better. He thought it best to say nothing about Andrew's threat to Watson and let whatever happened just happen.

After lunch, Jason was mopping the main bathrooms. He hated mopping the floors, but at least he could switch off and think he was somewhere else—think about Catherine, his father, and being home.

Andrew had garden duty. Some of the boys had to plant vegetables, mostly potatoes. Watson also worked out there with another four boys. Watson sat down on a sack of potatoes behind the potting shed. From a secret compartment behind a loose brick, he pulled out a metal tobacco tin, took out a cigarette and matches, and sat back smoking. His eyes closed as he dreamed of being in a far-off place—a place away from guards, locked doors, and windows with bars.

At first, he didn't felt the pain—just the thud against his chest. Then his eyes opened, and pain like he had never felt before burned across his chest. He focused his eyes.

Andrew was standing over him and smiling, with blood on his hands. He leaned forward and took the cigarette from Watson's mouth and placed it between his own smirking lips.

Watson gazed down at his body. A garden fork was sticking

out of his chest. His heart was punctured. He coughed a mouthful of blood onto his lap. He collapsed onto the ground, pushing the fork deeper into his body, which had now gone into spasms. He felt cold, light-headed. The pain finally went away.

Someone entered the bathroom, leaving a trail of dirty footprints. Jason looked up and saw the black shoe prints across the floor he had just cleaned. It woke him from his daydream.

"Hey, I just cleaned that," he said angrily. Then he stopped himself from saying any more.

What do I care? This whole place stinks anyway.

"Jason, clean it back up and wash this sink down," Andrew said, stripping his clothes off. He was splattered with blood. He collected clean clothes from the trash can. Once he washed his hands, he picked up the blood-stained clothes and took off with them. Jason cleaned the floor and sink as he was ordered.

An hour later, everyone was locked in their cells. The police had arrived and started a search. The juvenile center was in lockdown.

"They'll find the bloody clothes in Paul Jenkins's cell. When they interrogate you, just say he came into the bathroom and washed blood off his hands," Andrew ordered. Jason looked in disbelief.

"Is this why we have a lockdown? You killed Watson?"

"I told you he would be a corpse by tonight."

Jason felt cold, and he sat heavily on his bunk. If only he had told Governor Brown to move Watson, the boy would still be alive. A few hours passed before Andrew and Jason were taken to be interviewed in separate rooms.

"Jason Steed, I am Detective Spencer. Are you aware why you are here?"

"Shoplifting, sir."

"No, we know that. You are either stupid or you're testing me. Go ahead and test me if you want. Do you know why you are here in this office?"

"No, sir," Jason said nervously as he gripped the chair to try to stop shaking. It reminded him of the time when the military police had caught him playing on the flight simulator back in Hong Kong.

"A boy has been killed. Russell Watson. Do you know him?"

"I have seen him around, sir."

"Do you know who killed him?"

Jason had to make up his mind to either back Andrew or tell the truth. If he told the truth, he could go home and Andrew would stay locked up for years.

"Not sure, but I've got a good idea. I do all the mopping. I was in the bathroom and—" Jason paused.

"Go on, son. What happened?"

"I'm not a narc, sir. I can't say," Jason replied. He thought he had better play the part.

Detective Johnson stood up and walked around the table to Jason. He grabbed Jason by his overalls and got in his face. "Tell me, Steed, or it will get painful for you."

"You can't hurt me. You're the police. I know my rights. You can't touch me."

Spencer slammed his fist down on the desk in front of Jason. The loud bang made Jason jump. "You are a dirty, little thief. A common shoplifter. You don't have rights. What you *do* have is five seconds to tell me what you know." He raised his hand to grab Jason's neck.

Jason blocked it, jumped out of his seat, and stepped back ready to fight.

These are the police. Don't hurt them or you'll blow your cover.

"Okay, okay, I'll tell you. Just please don't hit me and don't tell anyone I narked." He raised his hands in surrender.

"Then sit," Spencer snapped.

"I was mopping the floors. I'd nearly finished when Paul Jenkins came in and tracked dirt across the clean floor. He got undressed and washed blood off his face and hands. Then he got dressed in new clothes and told me to clean up the sink. I did as I was told. He's a lot bigger than me, sir."

Jason's lies were believed. Paul Jenkins was arrested for killing Watson. The police also found the blood-stained clothes in his cell. Andrew was very pleased at the way it had turned out.

"They bought your story. Well done, Jason. You and I make a great team. I owe you," Andrew said, patting Jason on the back.

Perfect. You owe me, but when this is over, I will tell the truth.

CHAPTER 6

JASON WAS EXCITED THE following Saturday, as it was time for visitors. He kept watching the clock. Scott was coming, and he needed to tell him about Watson's death and how Andrew now owed him a favor. The inmates walked to the hall and stood in line.

"Your parents coming?" Jason asked Andrew.

Andrew nodded and smiled. It seemed strange to Jason that one minute Andrew was a cold-blooded killer and the next an excited schoolboy.

"Okay, boys, in you go. You know the rules," a guard shouted.

Jason was pleased to see Scott was not dressed up this time. He sat smiling at a table in the center, waiting for his friend to join him. They gave each other a hug and sat down. Scott watched out of the corner of his eye as Jason told him about Watson's murder and how he had lied to the police. He also told Scott about Boudica.

"You did the right thing, Jase. When this is over, you can tell the truth and they can have Cho on that too."

"Any news from George Young?" Jason asked.

There was none. Instead, Scott went on and on about SYUI headquarters and how he was there every night after school.

"School. I forgot about St. Joseph's. How is it?" Jason asked.

"I've been pushed around a bit now you're not there, but it'll be different when you're back. They've been told that you're sick."

"How are your parents?" Jason asked.

"Same. Dad's always working, and Mum, well, she seems happy. She asked about you."

"Your parents are cool, Scott."

"Your dad is pretty cool too, Jase. Although who knows what he will say when he finds out you did this against his wishes."

"I had no choice. You know that. George Young wanted me to help, and he made it pretty clear he gets his way. With Dad away, I had to decide. He must know by now. Mrs. Beeton was going to write and tell him, and I'm sure my grandparents are in a total panic. I hope they're not too upset."

"I suppose you haven't heard the news about Colin Wilkes at school?" Scott asked.

"What? 'Wilky'? Our future football superstar? Yeah, he was gonna get signed up for Manchester United as an apprentice."

"Not now. He failed a drug test, but I find it hard to believe."

"What? Wilky doing drugs? No way. He's a fitness freak and lives for football."

"It's true, Jase. Last weekend, he was arrested up in Manchester after a routine drug test. That's his football career over before it started."

"I still can't believe it. He must be devastated. What an idiot."

The hour visit was over in a flash. Again, Jason was depressed when he watched his friend leave—his only contact with his life away from this place.

After the visitors left, Andrew took Jason to one side.

"I told my dad about you. He said you may be able to work with us on the outside when we get out." It was the break Jason was looking for. Finally, this stupid plan was starting to pay off.

A social services worker waited outside the detention center for Jason. Four long weeks had past. Ms. Pettyfier was going to be Jason's social and probation officer. She wasn't in on the secret—all she knew was that Jason was a troubled boy who went from foster home to foster home until he had gotten locked up for shoplifting.

Ms. Pettyfier was a widow. She was tall and skinny, and she had long, greasy brown hair. She wore black-rimmed glasses and a long dark dress that hung off her stick-thin figure.

"I'll be in touch," Jason said to Andrew as they were leaving. Andrew was also being released, and his parents had just arrived to pick him up. As Jason walked down the corridor to meet Ms. Pettyfier, he smiled at Lin Cho, but the man just looked away as if Jason didn't exist. Jason followed Ms. Pettyfier to her car. She climbed in the driver's seat while he opened the passenger door.

"Um…what do you think you're doing?" she asked.

Is she joking or what?

"I thought you came to collect me, miss," Jason replied, bewildered.

"Children sit in the back, not the front," she snapped.

"Thanks for the big friendly welcome," Jason grunted, slamming the door shut and then climbing in the back.

"I can see how you got in trouble. You have an attitude problem. I only hope you snap out of it or else you'll be right back here." Jason sat in the back and silently mimicked her.

She drove painfully slow to a large apartment complex. Jason pressed his head up against the window and looked out at row upon row of identical houses. She parked her car where some scruffy boys were kicking a football.

"Miss, we use that wall as a goal," a small boy protested. His hair was messy. He had no front teeth, and he had holes in his vest.

"You will have to play elsewhere. I need to park my car," she snapped back at the boy.

"I can see why you choose this job. You are just *great* with kids!" Jason sniggered.

She looked down at him through her glasses and shook her head disapprovingly. The children watched as she walked him to the elevator.

A dirty sign hung at an angle with the words "Out of Order." So they climbed six flights of stairs that smelled like urine and walked along a balcony. She stopped at number 615, knocked on the door, and looked down at Jason.

"This is Mr. and Mrs. Bristow, a nice couple. They have looked after many children for us, and they are looking for a more permanent foster child. So if you behave and you all get along, I can't see any reason why you could not stay here permanently. They have one daughter, Janice, who's thirteen," Ms. Pettyfier explained.

Jason was dreading meeting new people and having to tell more lies, but the Triads may check into his background. SYUI could not risk them finding out Jason was actually a private school boy from a wealthy family. The door opened, and a girl not much taller than Jason appeared. She had long light brown hair tied in a ponytail. She wore jeans and a football shirt. She smiled, revealing braces.

"Hello, Ms. Pettyfier. This must be Jamie," she said happily.

"No, Janice, he's called Jason," she sniffed, walking through the doorway. Jason gave a weak smile to Janice and followed Ms. Pettyfier.

"Ah. M-M-M-Ms. Pettyfier. How are you? And this m-m-m-must be young Jason. Well, hello, young m-m-m-man. I'm Horace Bristow. It's a pleasure to m-m-m-meet you," he stuttered. "Veronica, dear, M-M-M-Ms. Pettyfier is here with Jason."

Mrs. Bristow came from the kitchen, smiling.

"Cup of tea, everyone?" she asked, and without waiting, she disappeared again. Jason took in his surroundings. The room was small, with an electric fireplace. There was a large brown couch with two matching armchairs and a small black-and-white TV on mute. In the corner, there were a table and four chairs. A few pictures of Janice growing up were in frames hanging on the wall.

They all sat at the table and drank tea. Janice stared at Jason, who kept his head down and wished he were somewhere else.

The following morning, Jason waited patiently outside the bathroom. Janice had been in there for half an hour, and he desperately needed to go.

What takes a girl so long? he said to himself. He looked at himself in the full-length mirror that was fixed to a wall in the narrow hall. His blond bangs swept across his eyes, and his hair was a mess. His new pajamas were creased and unbuttoned. He looked quite small, standing almost cross-legged.

What is taking her so long? I'm gonna piss myself in a minute.

Finally, she came out. She paused and turned slightly red when she saw Jason in his pajamas.

His first day of school went well. He enjoyed going to a mixed school for a change.

"May I go out after dinner? I've done my homework." Jason smiled. Mr. and Mrs. Bristow looked at each other.

"Where do you want to go? We'll take you," Mrs. Bristow suggested.

"Nowhere. Just fresh air and take a look around the area. I'll be home before nine."

"No, nine is too late, Jason," Mr. Bristow replied. "We will m-m-m-m-make it eight, but stay close. Janice can show you around."

Janice gave her father a filthy look. She had her own plans, and they did not include baby-sitting Jason.

Once outside the apartment, Janice spoke abruptly to Jason. "Look, you don't want to hang with me and I don't want to hang with you. Don't get me wrong. I like you. You're cute for a little brother, but I have my own friends. I'll meet you downstairs at eight. Don't you *dare* be late."

Anchor Avenue was two miles away. It took Jason fifteen minutes to run there. He came to number 62, which was one of the largest homes on the street. The large, brick house had bay windows and a neatly manicured garden. A black Rolls-Royce was parked on the drive, and next to that was a black Land Rover.

Jason rang the doorbell and waited until an elderly Chinese man answered.

"Hello, I'm Jason. I've come to see Andrew."

The man waved Jason into the hallway and closed the door. "Andrew, you have a visitor," the old man shouted in Chinese.

"Who is it?" Andrew's voice shouted back in Chinese from upstairs. The old man had gone into the kitchen and didn't reply. Andrew, wearing just his white school shirt and underwear, appeared and looked down the stairs.

"Oh, it's you, Jason. Well, you'd better come up."

"You don't seem too pleased to see me. Is everything all right?" Jason questioned as he ran up the stairs.

"Yeah," Andrew assured him, performing a slow-motion high kick toward Jason.

"You did say I could come by and you would get me a job with your father when we got out."

"Did he now?" Lin Cho said behind Jason. Jason was taken by surprise. He turned to see Cho right behind him, his arms folded. He was wearing a black suit and tie that looked too small for his slightly overweight figure.

"Andrew, where is your honor? You have a guest. Put some clothing on," he ordered.

"It's only Jason, Father. We shared a cell. He's seen a lot more than this. He's the boy I told you about. He could be of some use."

"You're a little on the small side, but Andrew speaks highly of you. A Western boy as a lookout could be useful."

"What's my size got to do with it? I can take anyone you or Andrew can," Jason said firmly.

"Andrew is a black belt and a great fighter. I myself am a black belt second dan. I doubt that you could match us."

Jason bit his lip. He had over six years of karate and judo training. At age five, he had competed against boys who were ten and older, and they all had been twice his weight and size. Now, he could fight an adult opponent as easily as anyone else.

How many more times have I got to prove myself?

Jason followed Andrew into his room. It had "welcome home" cards stuck on one wall and posters of Bruce Lee on the others, which was very similar to Jason's own room back home.

"I want you to come with me Saturday, Jason. I have some unfinished business," Andrew said, passing Jason a can of Coke.

"What sort of business?"

"There's a small store just off the high street. The owner refused to pay me. He was the guy I was beating up when the police showed up. I'm positive he called them in advance. Father has not collected anything since. He's left it for me to deal with."

"So he owes your father quite a bit of back money?" Jason quizzed.

"No, it's not money anymore. He has blown that chance. This is personal. If I am to be number two in my father's organization, I will need to get respect. I have to make an example of him. We're going to kill him," he said coldly.

Jason took a long drink from his can, trying to think of something to say. He had to go along with it, but he could not be part of murder.

"I've got to go. These new foster parents gave me a curfew."

"The Bristows. I'll drive you," Andrew said and jumped off the bed and pulled on his shoes.

"How did you know their name?" Jason gasped.

"Jason, my father is deputy mountain master of the Triads.

Have you heard of the Wo Shing Wo? That's our Triad name. He is one step away from Boudica. Boudica is dragon leader. We have to be careful who we allow in. We've checked you out. It's just a precaution."

"Did I pass the test when you checked me out?"

"You're still breathing, aren't you?"

CHAPTER 7

JASON HAD ARRANGED TO meet Scott the following night at the park. It was planned for every third day at the same time. After he found out that the Triads had checked him out, he was concerned for Scott's safety. He was also concerned for the Bristows' safety. It may have been smart to use a real foster family for cover, but now they were in danger. He got to the park early and watched the direction he knew Scott would be coming in.

Jason sat on a swing and glanced at his watch—ten past six. They had arranged to meet at six. He wondered if Scott was still coming. He finally showed up and joined Jason on the swings. To anyone watching, it was just two boys rocking on the swings and talking. You would never guess they were passing information about murder plots.

"Your grandparents are down from Scotland and have flipped out. They gave Mrs. Beeton a hard time *and* they came around to my house. Your gran is really upset. I had to call George Young or she was going to call the police."

"Oh, no, what did he do?"

"He told them it was a matter for SYUI and British security and that if they tried to make a fuss, they could be putting you in danger. They're staying at your house. Oh, and they called the admiralty and spoke to your father. As you can guess, he is pretty mad with George Young and you."

"Jesus, what a mess. I will be in for it when this is over and he gets home. I feel sorry for Mrs. Beeton. Get a message to my grandparents. Tell them I'm fine and they are to apologize to Mrs. Beeton. She's just the housekeeper. It's not her fault, and let's face it, she couldn't have stopped me."

Scott stopped his swing and stood and faced Jason, who had to drag his feet on the ground to stop before he knocked Scott over.

"You want *me* to go around to your house and face your grandparents? They'll skin me alive! Those Scottish people are weird."

"Hey, my mum was Scottish. Take that back. Just tell Gran I sent my love and she'll be cool."

"Oh, sorry, I didn't mean anything bad about your mum. Okay, I'll go and see them, but if you don't ever see me again, you'll know they cut me up and stuck me in a haggis."

Jason grinned at Scott. They started walking over to the jungle gym, which was shaped like an igloo with metal bars. Jason jumped up and lifted his legs. Once he was hanging upside down by his legs, he continued, "Now down to work. On Saturday, Andrew Cho and I are going to kill a guy—the same guy he was assaulting when he was arrested and caught by the police. He wants to send a message that he's the big grown-up son of Lin Cho. How do I get out of it without breaking my cover? I can't kill a guy or watch it happen."

"Dunno. I'll ask George Young and see what he says. What's your new school like?" Scott panted as he climbed up. He wasn't as brave as Jason and thought better of hanging upside down by just his legs.

"Easy, relaxed. They don't have a 'Taffy' Griffiths. It's a coed school, so it's different having girls in the class. But no one is as pretty as Catherine. I wish I could call her."

"As much as I like working at SYUI and being the messenger, I will be glad when this is over. A few guys at school have started pushing me around. You know, the usual stuff, calling me a nerd."

"You are a nerd, Scott. That's what I like about you." Jason laughed.

Scott cursed at Jason and punched his leg, almost causing Jason to fall. "I can't think why I like you. Probably because it makes me feel superior because of your lack of intelligence."

"Probably." Jason smiled. Scott looked back and smiled at his friend. They climbed off the frame and toward the grass when two smaller boys came to play on the bars.

"Well, actually, there is some news about school, but it's not good. Colin Wilkes hanged himself two days ago."

"What? No way! Why?" Jason was shocked by the news. They had not been close friends but had often run track together after school.

"Probably because he was a junky and got kicked out of Man U."

"Wilky wasn't a junky," Jason said.

"Well, he failed the drug test and then he went into a deep depression. Sorry, mate, it's true."

The following morning, Janice was arguing with her mother. She was upset that there were not any Coco-Bites left. First she blamed Jason for eating them until her mother reminded her that she had eaten them herself after school. She left for school early without saying good-bye and slammed the front door behind her.

"Did I cause that?" Jason asked.

"No, dear, she is at that age when she knows best. For some reason, she can't stop eating that cereal. I notice you don't eat it," Mrs. Bristow said, trying to straighten Jason's school tie as he was putting his shoes on.

"I prefer just milk for breakfast. I like to run to school, and I can't do that on a full stomach," he said, picking up his schoolbag.

Jason started jogging to school along the road, and a man in running shorts came up alongside him.

"Hello, boyo. I'm with George Young. Take Wilkinson Avenue," the man said with a broad Welsh accent. He then increased speed and ran on ahead.

As Jason turned into Wilkinson Avenue, he looked for George. The street was heavily lined with trees and full of parked cars. A black van drove alongside him. When Jason noticed it out of the corner of his eye, it slowed down to his speed.

It's got to be SYUI.

Without even looking, he ran into the street and the side door opened. As it slowed, Jason jumped in and the door was closed behind him.

"Jason Steed, good morning, mate. How are ya? Your bleeding grandmother got in a right state over you, she did. She was gonna go and call the 'Old Bill,'" George said happily. Jason smiled at George and shook his hand. George was overweight and always smelled of body odor and cigarettes.

"I take it you got my message about Saturday," Jason panted.

"Yeah, a bit of a problem…that. Do you know what they're raising the money for yet?"

"No, but what do I do about Saturday?"

"You've gotta do it. I know you can kill with your bare hands. You proved yourself in Jakarta. How many did you kill then? Five or six? Although you shot some, so that don't count."

Jason cursed under his breath. "You *are* joking? I can't kill some shopkeeper!"

"I don't want you to kill him—just make it look like it. Kick him around a bit. Behind the counter will be a 'prop knife.' Stab him with it." The van came to a stop.

"What's a prop knife?" Jason asked, concerned.

"It's what the actors use on films. It's telescopic, so it won't stab him. It will fold up, and a small capsule of animal blood will burst open. Makes a right bloody mess but looks like the real McCoy. Actors normally get a chance to practice. You don't. You got one shot. The shopkeeper is counting on you with his life. Although to be honest, he doesn't know about it."

"What if it doesn't work and Andrew wants to kill him?"

"You'd better get out, Jason, or you'll be late for school."

"You didn't answer my question."

"There you go now. Remember, it will be behind the counter," George said, opening the door, putting his hand on Jason's shoulder, and nudging him out. Jason pulled his arm away. "Come on. You'll be late for school."

"I'm not getting out until you answer my question. What do I do? Andrew may even have a gun. Do I stop Andrew or let him murder someone?"

Again, George tried to push Jason out the van. This time, Jason caught George's hand and bent his fingers back hard. George slipped off his seat in pain and tried to free his fingers.

"Tell me what to do."

"Okay, let me bloody fingers go," George shouted. "Everyone, out. I need to talk to Jason." The driver and man next to him in the front seat climbed out and shut the doors. George sat back and clenched his fingers. He pulled out a cigarette and lit it.

"Jason, I'm really sorry to put you in a spot like this, mate. At your age, you should be in school, thinking about girls and football. But we believe the Triads are up to something very big—so big it will go down in history. I can't answer your question. We *have* to have a lead. I am depending on you to get it for us. If someone gets hurt or killed, well, there are bigger things at stake. I've got your back." George took out a tissue and wiped his forehead. Jason noticed how worried he looked. He had lost his cocky smile and arrogance. He was a man who looked terrified of the consequences.

Early Saturday morning, Andrew stood outside the Bristows', dressed in black. He had a pair of black leather gloves, and his jet-black hair shone in the morning sunlight.

"You look like Bruce Lee in *Enter the Dragon*," Jason joked when he approached. Andrew said nothing as he walked past Jason. He knew his father would be watching today's events, and he was certain that Boudica would also hear about it. Today was business. He had to act responsibly and take care of his reputation. Jason followed close to his side.

After a short bus ride, Jason followed Andrew off the bus and down a small street. It was a poor neighborhood. Many of the homes were in need of repair. Old cars that had clearly seen better days were parked alongside the pavement. Andrew stopped and bent down. He was pretending to tie his shoelaces.

"That's it—there," Andrew said, nodding toward the corner store. An elderly lady was coming out. She had a wicker basket on wheels, and they watched as she wrapped a scarf around her neck and slowly walked away. Andrew marched on toward the store.

As they entered, a bell rang. It was a small shop that sold prepackaged food, milk, tobacco products, and newspapers. Jason took in his surroundings: A counter was at the far end, with a cash register to the right. On the back wall, large jars of various colored candy and toffee filled a shelf. There was a small door opening behind the counter, and music was playing.

An old bald man came from behind the counter and smiled at Jason. He was stooped over and wore wire-framed glasses.

"Good morning, young man. How can I help you?" he asked.

It's now or never. Sorry, but this will save your life.

Jason spun on one leg. His foot shot out in a perfectly timed full roundhouse kick that slammed into the soft flesh of the man's stomach. Jason changed feet and carried out a second attack, kicking him twice in the chest and pushing him back behind the counter. With all the wind knocked out of him, the shopkeeper collapsed behind the counter and gasped for air. Jason scanned frantically behind the counter, searching for the knife.

Where is it?

As the shopkeeper tried to get to his feet again, Jason kicked him. He lunged forward and thrust his knee onto the old man's chest, pinning his victim down. He saw the knife out of the corner of his eye and scooped it up. It was cold and heavy to the touch. Jason's fingers wrapped around the handle and brought the knife down hard onto the man's chest. The man cried out in pain, and blood spat back into Jason face. His hand was covered with blood as he climbed off his prey. Andrew looked over the counter. Jason bent down to feel a pulse on the man's neck. Nothing.

"I can't feel a pulse," Jason announced in shock.

"Come on. We'd better go," Andrew ordered.

"I can't feel a pulse," Jason said again, panic now setting in.

"That's the whole idea, Jase. Good work. Now come on. Let's go."

Jason followed Andrew out of the store. He was dazed, panting and sweating. Jason had killed before—an enemy on Jakarta— but that has been a war zone. This was an English civilian—just an old man like his grandfather. Andrew stopped and took off his jacket. He wiped Jason's face with his hand and placed his jacket around Jason. He could see Jason was in shock. This was one time Jason didn't need to act.

The bus ride back to Andrew's home was a hazy dream to Jason. When they got off the bus and started to walk, he kneeled down and threw up. Andrew helped him to his feet.

As they entered Andrew's home, Lin Cho was waiting in the hallway with his driver/bodyguard, Kotang. Kotang stood nearly seven feet tall; he was so wide that he had to turn his shoulders to get through most doors. He had once been a Japanese sumo wrestler, but after he had murdered a woman in Japan, he had fled to Great Britain. Cho looked at Andrew as they entered. He noticed that Jason was covered in blood.

"Is he all right? You should not have taken him. He is too small. I knew he would get hurt."

"No, Father, he's fine. Jason killed him. It was his first kill, and he's just shaken up," Andrew said as he took Jason to the kitchen. Cho and Kotang followed.

"*Jason* killed him? It seems you have found a worthy friend. A boy with his looks, a Westerner, could be very useful to us." Cho grinned. Jason pulled off his shirt and stuck his head under the flow of cold water. He watched the water turn red as it washed the blood off his face. When he was clean, he dried off. He faced Andrew.

"Did I do all right, Andrew?"

"Yes and no. I never told you to kill him. You were supposed to keep watch. But, damn, you were so fast!"

"Boys, I am going to see Boudica in an hour, and I would like you two to join us." This was the break Jason had been hoping to get—a chance to meet Boudica.

CHAPTER 8

ANDREW SMILED AT JASON. They both sat in the back of Lin Cho's Rolls-Royce on their way to see Boudica. Andrew told Jason to keep the black leather jacket because it suited him.

Jason didn't reply. He was still thinking about the shopkeeper. He couldn't feel a pulse! Maybe he had been feeling in the wrong place? He told himself that had to be it. The knife was there just as George had said. It must have been a fake knife with animal blood.

They eventually came to a large industrial park. At the far end was a huge, dirty building with many other buildings connected to it. Trucks drove in and out of the large, guarded gates. An eight-foot fence topped with barbed wire surrounded the entire compound. Security cameras were mounted every forty feet. Jason noticed security guards with guard dogs patrolling the perimeter inside and outside.

"Is this a prison?" Jason asked.

Cho and Kotang laughed at his remark.

"This is Boudica's factory. Have you heard of 'B Food Company, Ltd.'?" Andrew asked.

Jason paused and thought as the car stopped at the front gates.

"I think so. Don't they make breakfast cereal?"

"Yes, the top selling brand is Coco-Bites. Boudica owns the company. She is the 'B' in 'B Food Company.'"

Jason looked confused. *If she was head of the Triads, why would she also own a children's breakfast company?*

Kotang drove up to the large building. The once-red brick-work had turned black over the years with grime from London's smog and pollution. The tiny windows had bars across them. Inside was just as dark and gloomy. As they entered, Jason could taste sugar in the atmosphere and a strong, pleasant smell. It reminded him of his kitchen at home after Mrs. Beeton had been making his favorite food: carrot cake.

Large stainless steel containers of flour and sugar with connecting pipes filled the interior. Workers with white coats, gloves, and blue hard hats walked briskly and checked various dials and gauges.

Pallets of cereal boxes were stacked from floor to ceiling. Forklift trucks loaded with boxes and various supplies sped around. A conveyor belt carried what Jason could only describe as thousands of cereal boxes.

They walked up a large metal stairway and followed a walkway suspended from the ceiling to an office at the end.

"Boudica, how are you?" Cho smiled and bowed.

Behind a desk sat a figure. Jason looked and made eye contact. She stood and glanced at him. She was slender and tall, Chinese with blond hair. Her skin was white and looked pale compared to her bright red lips. She had dark, intelligent eyes and wore a tight-fitting purple silk dress cut above the knee. As she walked around the desk to shake Lin's hand, Jason watched her. She had a large slit on the side of her dress, and as she walked, it opened and slid so high that Jason was sure it would reveal her underwear. Her glossy black boots with large heels made her look even taller than she actually was.

She looked down at Cho. "I understand Andrew took care of a little problem with his new friend," she spoke in Chinese.

"Yes, Andrew has gained his reputation back. This will make our clients think next time," Lin answered in Chinese.

"There had better not be a next time. This pretty boy—I don't trust Westerners—why would you bring him here?" she said scornfully.

"He will be helpful to us. *He* actually killed the problem and helped Andrew in juvie. I've had him checked out. He's harmless. As you know, the police and SYUI are watching our every move. They would never suspect a boy like him to be working for us. Plus, he's now a killer." Lin smiled.

"Come here, boy," she ordered. Jason ignored the remark. As far as they were concerned, he didn't speak Chinese. Andrew looked at Jason and nodded his head toward Boudica.

"What?" asked Jason in English.

Boudica smiled at him, her eyes still showing no emotion. "Come here, boy," she repeated in English.

"The name is Steed. Jason Steed, miss," he said as he approached. "You must be Boudica." He held out his hand.

"Are you not afraid of me, *boy*?" she asked. Jason pulled his hand away as she put hers out. She was standing with her hand outstretched, furious.

"My name is Jason Steed."

Cho raised his eyes. Andrew held his breath. Boudica looked shocked. Clearly outraged, she turned and went back behind her desk.

"We are already at full production. My plant in the United States will open next month. Within a year, I shall be the richest woman in China and will never have to smell this rotten stench again. The money will go back to our homeland, and I will once and for all rid China of Chairman Mao. China will be a great country again, and *I*, Boudica, shall be its queen. The stupid Western children and their addiction will provide me with everything I need to overthrow him." She admired her long red fingernails and continued, "I have a place for you, Lin Cho. You have done very well. You and your family will be rewarded beyond your wildest dreams." She laughed.

Jason started to shake nervously. What he had heard did not make much sense, but it was important he let George know. His ability to speak Chinese had been invaluable. It now made sense why SYUI had chosen him.

"Jason Steed, it was…amusing to meet you. I have never met someone so small and yet so confident before. You are right to be proud of your name. I apologize for calling you *boy*." She held out her hand. Jason walked forward and shook it. It felt cold and stiff.

"Lin Cho, you and the boys have arrived just in time. We captured a spy and have him downstairs. They are interrogating him now. You must all come and meet him," she said, pleased. They followed Boudica down the staircase, and the workers in the blue overalls bowed their heads. It sickened Jason.

They followed Boudica into a room that was like a hospital operating room. A man was strapped down to the bed, half-naked. Two Chinese men in white coats who looked like twins stood over him. Jason took in his surroundings.

"This is Officer Jim Kinver with SYUI. He has been spying on me. But now Jim has nothing to say. Well, Wing and Wong will get him chatting."

Cho walked up to the bed and slapped Kinver across the face.

"Why are you watching us? What do you know?" Jim turned his head and looked away. He briefly made eye contact with Jason. Cho picked up a surgeon's knife and cut a line across Kinver's chest. He screamed out in pain. Jason and Andrew flinched at the bloody sight and sound of his screams. Kinver then had a gag put across his mouth by one of the twins to prevent him from screaming. Boudica walked across and picked up a pair of wire cutters.

"Are you ready to talk yet, Jimmy boy?" she asked.

He glared at her and struggled against the leather ties that held down his hands and feet. His body fought like a wild animal trying to free itself from a trap. Without a second thought, Boudica cut off the small finger on his right hand. Blood shot out across the floor. One of the twins lit a blowtorch and scorched the stub to prevent him from bleeding to death. His sweat-covered face was racked with pain. He screamed against the gag. Jason felt like throwing up. He wasn't sure he could watch any more.

"Tell us who else is involved or loose a toe!" Cho shouted.

Kinver again looked at Jason, who was trying to look away.

"I'm working alone," Kinver protested. "I suspected that you are running a protection scheme. That's all!"

Cho laughed and said, "They don't send in SYUI for a small issue like a protection racket. You are lying. Good-bye, little toes."

Kinver screamed as Cho removed a toe on his left foot. The

pain from the blowtorch was worse. Jason's stomach churned as the room was consumed with the stench of burning flesh. Boudica looked at Jason. She tilted her head and studied him.

"How rude of us, Jason. We are having all the fun," she said, licking a spot of Kinver's blood off her long white fingernail. "It's your turn now."

"No, thanks. I've already killed once today. No need to be greedy. You carry on. I'll watch," he said nervously, forcing a smile.

"It was an order, not a request," Boudica snapped back. Jason paused. His brain was churning, trying to figure a way out.

I could take Lin and Andrew. I'm certain Boudica would be easy, the two twins probably as well, but Kotang is outside. He would snap me in half! I can't risk fighting them all alone. If I lose, it'll be me strapped to the bed, and that won't help Kinver.

He walked up to the bed, desperately trying to think of something. Jason picked up a knife and put it back down. He then picked up a pillow off the floor.

"That won't hurt him enough to make him speak, Jase," Andrew scoffed.

Jason pulled off the pillowcase, folded it up tight, and placed it over Kinver's face and nose. After thirty seconds, Kinver fought back, trying desperately to breathe, his face turning blue. Finally, Jason removed it.

"You'd better tell them what they want know. I'm new to this, and next time, I may do it too long," Jason said quietly. Kinver's eyes glared at Jason in total disbelief.

"Come on, Jason. It's my turn," Andrew said, trying to act tough in front of the others. Jason again pushed the pillowcase across his mouth and nose. The others in the room didn't notice Jason's fingers feeling Kinver's neck just below his right ear. Once Jason found the right pressure point, he pushed down, and this blocked the blood to the brain. After a few seconds, Kinver was unconscious. Jason pulled the pillowcase away.

"Oops. Looks like I've killed two today…sorry."

Boudica gestured one of the twins to check Kinver.

"He is alive but fainted," he told Boudica in Chinese.

"You killed him, Jason," she lied. Jason decided to play along.

"Good. Anyone who is a threat to Andrew and his family deserves to be dead." Jason frowned.

"He's not really dead. He's just fainted. You're a cold-hearted little brat. I like that."

CHAPTER 9

J ASON WALKED BACK INTO the Bristows' flat. He wanted to contact George, but he was unsure if he was being followed. As he entered the living room, all eyes stared at him. Janice shook her head and looked away.

"Has someone died?" he sniggered.

"It's not a laughing m-m-m-matter, Jason. We are trying to be flexible, but you have been gone all day. And why is your shirt bloody?" Mr. Bristow said as he stood. He walked over to Jason. "I don't want to be heavy-handed, Jason. We all like you. But if I have to install discipline, I will."

"I was at the park all day playing football. Met some new friends. Then some small kid fell off the slide. I helped him until his parents came to fetch him. I think they took him to the hospital," Jason said, trying to look hurt. Mr. and Mrs. Bristow now looked very guilty for not trusting him.

Maybe I overdid it.

Janice watched through squinted eyes silently. She clearly did not believe his story, but Jason had bigger things to worry about. He had to get word to George urgently.

Jason lay in bed. The hall light that shone under the crack of his bedroom door went out. He decided he would wait a while for the Bristows to fall sleep and then sneak out. After twenty minutes, he climbed out of bed and started getting dressed when suddenly his door opened. He fell as he tried to quickly get back into his bed and under the covers.

"What are you up to?" Janice whispered.

"Nothing. What are you doing in here?" Jason hissed, trying to hide the fact that he was only wearing one sock and his underwear.

"Nothing? Then why aren't you in your pajamas?"

"I'm not tired. I don't burst into your room. I respect your privacy. Now please respect mine and get out."

"Not until you tell me what you're up to." She picked up the odd sock off the floor and sat on his bed with her arms folded.

"I'm not up to nothing. Just go," Jason said, trying to pry his sock out of her grasp.

"You lied to my parents tonight. I don't know what you're up to, but I won't let my parents get hurt. You're not going out this time of night, are you?" Janice whispered. "Then I'm coming with you."

"Out of the question."

"I'll call my parents." She stood, and with her arms still folded, she looked at him with her eyebrows raised, questioning him.

I'm glad I don't have a nosey sister in my real life.

They crept out of the apartment and ran down the flights of stairs.

"What's the rush?" she asked, almost running to keep up with his brisk walking speed.

"The buses will stop running soon." Once they arrived at the bus stop, Jason read the timetable and realized the last bus had left at ten. He took Janice by the arm and started running.

They came to a pub, and outside, a row of taxis were waiting for customers. Jason opened the back door and jumped in and pulled Janice with him.

"You kids are out bloody late. Where have you been?" the taxi driver asked.

"A party. Church road, South London. And we're late, so make it quick please," Jason ordered. Janice sat back and looked at Jason while he continued to give address details.

The taxi pulled up outside Scott's home, and Jason climbed out.

"Janice will wait here until I get your money. How much do we owe you, sir?" Jason asked.

"Six quid, mate."

Jason rang the bell at the Turners' house and rattled the letter box at the same time. The second time he rang the bell, the lights came on in the house. The door slowly opened, and Dr. Turner peered around the crack, wearing his dressing gown and slippers. His hair was sticking up like he'd been electrocuted.

"Dr. Turner, I need six pounds to pay the taxi," Jason asked, gesturing with his head at the taxi. The clackity diesel engine smothered the silence of the night.

The Turners were like a second family to Jason. They knew he was working for SYUI and that Scott was the contact. Nothing Jason did surprised them now. Dr. Turner waddled down the path and plucked banknotes from his wallet. Jason ran upstairs to Scott's room and quietly entered.

Scott was lying on his back, fast asleep. Jason sat quietly on Scott's bed and placed a hand over his mouth and pinched his friend's nose closed with his other hand. After a few seconds, Scott woke up struggling to breathe, twisting his head from side to side, trying to remove the obstruction.

"What? Who's there?" Scott asked, still half asleep.

"Hello, mate. Wake up. I need your help." Jason laughed. Scott cursed at him. "There's no need to use that language. I've come to see you."

"Thanks for the gentle shake to wake me up." He cursed again. His bedroom light went on. Dr. Tuner came in, and he was followed by Janice.

"Who's she?" Scott asked.

"Scott, this is Janice. Janice, this is Scott. I've some news, and it can't wait. We need to inform George Young...now."

Jason stood up and pulled the covers off of Scott.

"Get dressed, Scott. Jim Kinver could be dead by tomorrow. We need to act now. Dr. Turner, can you drive us to Scotland Yard please?"

"I don't think I have much of a choice, but won't that blow your cover if you are seen?"

"It's a chance I'll have to take. Scott, get dressed," Jason said sternly.

"But there's a girl in my room," Scott whined, pulling the sheet over himself.

Thirty minutes later in a large office full of desks, typewriters, telephones, and files of paper, George stood in front of his assembled team. Most looked like they had just gotten out of bed—some dressed as if they had been out for the evening and not yet got home. He marched toward Jason and shook his hand.

"Good to see you again, cocker. I hear you survived the corner

61

shop incident. Well done. I knew you would." George was sweating and smelled of body odor as normal. Tonight his breath smelled of garlic too. George turned and shook Scott's hand.

Then he sat down behind a desk and looked at the two boys. They looked tiny among the high-ranking SYUI officers. All the officers had been recruited from the metropolitan police and all stood at over six foot.

Jason started to turn red and looked at Scott with a painful expression.

"Jase, tell them what you found out," Scott whispered. Jason took a deep breath. He looked directly at George and tried to block out the others in the room.

"Jim Kinver. They've caught him, and he will probably be dead by the morning if we don't get him out tonight," Jason said quietly.

"What'd he say?" an officer at the back of the office shouted.

"Speak up. Stand on a chair or something," another suggested.

Jason turned bright red and nervously started to shake.

What's wrong with me? Jason asked himself.

He had never before spoken to a large group and was surprised with himself that he couldn't do it. Scott looked at him and was surprised to notice he was so nervous. He had always seen Jason as his fearless hero. For the first time, he saw Jason in a different light. Jason had stage fright! Scott leaned forward and whispered in Jason's ear.

"I read that if you imagine the audience naked, it's easy to talk." As he listened to Scott's advice, Jason peered around the room and then looked at George.

"Yuck, that's gross," Jason said, pulling a face like he was going to be sick. He walked over to George and pulled a chair next to him. George looked at Jason, and like Scott, he was surprised to see Jason was nervous and shaking.

"So you are human after all. Okay, son, tell me." George smiled. As Jason spoke to George, a hum of conversation went around the room.

After five minutes, George thanked Jason and stood up and walked to the center of the room. Scott joined Jason.

"Jim Kinver's been caught. He's been bloody tortured. It sounds pretty horrific. He has lost fingers and toes. If it wasn't for Jason, he would probably be 'brown bread' by now, but as far as we know, he's still alive and kicking."

"He won't be kicking much with no toes," Scott sniggered. In return, he got a look that could kill from Jason. He immediately knew that had been in bad taste. "Sorry, Jase." Jason shook his head disapprovingly at his friend.

George continued and explained everything. For the next hour, Jason had to make a detailed statement. He explained everything. They could not figure out how Boudica could possibly be selling enough cereal to fund a takeover of the Chinese government.

By three in the morning with no fresh ideas, SYUI officers started to lose interest. They doubted some of what Jason had told them. Scott took Jason to the cafeteria to get a drink. They wanted to try to stay awake. Dr. Turner and Janice were already there, sitting at a table and drinking hot chocolate.

"Is it over? Can we go home now?" Dr. Turner asked.

"No, Dr. Turner. Sorry." Jason said as he sat down heavily in a chair next to Janice. Scott was at the counter. The cafeteria was open twenty-four hours for the police who came on and off duty. He collected a tray with some food and drink and joined them.

"Will someone tell me what's going on? Jason—if that is your real name—are you in trouble?" Janice asked.

"Yes, my real name is Jason Steed. For now, that's all I can say." She was not happy with the answer. She folded her arms across her chest and turned away.

"Here, mate, I got us a Coke and a bowl of Coco-Bites each." Scott smiled.

"Thanks, I'll have the Coke, but I won't eat Coco-Bites. They are made by Boudica's company. I want nothing to do with that witch," Jason said as he pulled the tab off a can of Coke.

"I'll have them then." Janice said, swiftly taking the bowl. She and Scott hungrily ate the cereals.

"Looks like they haven't eaten in weeks," Dr. Turner said and laughed. "He is getting through three boxes a week."

"That's nothing. I have a friend at school that eats a box a day," Janice replied with a mouthful. "She is addicted to them more than me."

Scott stopped eating, gazed at his bowl, and then looked at Jason. Jason looked back quite confused by Scott's look. Scott was in deep thought. He repeated what Janice said. "Addicted to them. Is that what you said?" He kept his gaze on Jason's eyes. His brain was working overtime. Jason blinked and tried to look away from the stare that was getting uncomfortable.

"Are you two going to kiss or what?" Janice questioned. Scott continued to stare blankly into Jason's eyes. Eventually he got up and went back to the counter and picked up a box of Coco-Bites and studied it. He looked up at Jason, who was watching him.

"*Got it!*" he shouted. "Come on." Jason followed Scott back up the stairs to the SYUI office.

"Are you sure you have worked it out, Scott? They made me look pretty stupid," Jason said, walking behind with his hands in his pockets.

"*They* are the stupid ones."

George and the others were talking, trying to decide if they should rescue Kinver and blow the case. They had given up on Jason. Scott burst into the room.

"Mr. Young, Jason's right. I know how Boudica will get the money." Jason sat next to George while Scott stood at the front of the room and held the box of Coco-Bites.

"How many boxes per week are sold in Britain?" Scott asked.

The officers sighed. Was this a boy's game? They were now being treated like schoolchildren. George groaned until Jason kicked him under the table.

"I thought SYUI stood for Scotland Yard Undercover Intelligence. Then show me some intelligence. Come on…how many?" Scott repeated. Jason watched Scott full of admiration. He had no idea what Scott was about to say but had full confidence in him.

"Maybe one hundred thousand," George replied.

"No. Wrong. Try ten million and growing," Scott said.

"What the bloody hell has this to do with anything?" George shouted.

"Who owns the company?" Scott asked.

"Yes, we know. Boudica," a female officer interrupted.

"So, when she doubles the price or even triples it, that's an extra twenty or thirty million per week. That is just the UK. Jason has already told us that she is opening a plant in America. Once the Americans start eating them—and let's not forget there are over two hundred million Americans—we can add another six hundred million per day. In a week, that's enough money to buy some corrupt politicians, feed an army, and have some change. She will be the richest woman in China. She will control everything she wants. She will be able to overthrow the Mao government." Scott rolled his sleeves up and pushed his hair back over his head.

"What are you saying, Scott?" George asked.

"Have you tried these?" Scott asked.

"No, but my son eats them. Actually, he eats a lot of them—bloody addicted to the stuff."

"Exactly. And no doubt if the price was to double or triple, you would still buy them to keep him happy," Scott said with his arms folded. He looked at Jason and smiled. George put his arms up, looking for an explanation.

"So, you think she is just going to sell a few boxes of cereal? But that's not illegal!" George shouted.

"But the secret ingredient in Coco-Bites is what? It's nothing new really. When they started making Coca-Cola back in 1895—when you were still a boy—they actually put a few milligrams of cocaine in the ingredients. That and the caffeine made it slightly addictive—but nothing like whatever they are putting in Coco-Bites. It's must be a new secret ingredient that keeps people addicted. This way, people won't be able to stop buying them at any price."

"They can't put bloody secret ingredients in kid's cereal." He got up, took the box off Scott, and threw it to a man sitting behind him. "Take it to the lab and test it," George demanded. He stood up and shouted orders. They were going to raid Boudica's yard as soon as they got the test results. "Scott!" he shouted. "What the bloody hell did you mean? In 1895, when I was a boy? To you, I may seem old, but I am not that old." He grinned and winked at the boys.

CHAPTER 10

As the sun broke, the gray London sky slowly appeared above the rooftops of row upon row of houses. TV antennas pointed south, attached to smokeless chimneys that lined up in a never-ending row of disorganized modern architecture. George nudged Jason to wake up. They were outside Boudica's compound. SYUI wanted Jason to join the raid, as he knew where Kinver was being held. Although George had a secret agenda, he wanted to witness for himself Jason in action.

Jason yawned and slowly opened an eye. He snuggled under what he thought was a blanket. He looked down. It was George's jacket. He must have placed it on him after Jason had gone to sleep.

He does have a heart after all.

"What time is it?" Jason yawned, stretching his arms and shivering.

"Just after six. They just called us on the radio. Scott was right. Coco-Bites is loaded with special sugars and chemicals that attach themselves to our bodies' nervous systems. That's why you kids are addicted to it. The stuff works like a super dose of caffeine and illegal drugs. If you stopped eating the cereal, you would go through withdraw. It would give headaches and cause depression."

"Don't look at me. I don't touch it, but I bet that's what killed a friend of mine. Colin Wilkes, he must have been eating it before they gave him a drug test. He ended up killing himself after being thrown off the Manchester United second team. Boudica is responsible for that too. That witch has a lot to answer for."

When Jason climbed out of the car and removed George's jacket, the cold air flushed over his stiff body and he tried to flex his muscle to get some warm blood pumping around. George gave orders on the radio. Everyone was to stand and wait for his signal.

"Okay, Jason, where is he?"

"That building on the right. We need to get to him before this lot comes crushing through the gates." Jason pointed with his finger.

"Easier said than done. That building is the farthest away from the gates. How do we get that far before the guards come out?"

"Drive in and leave the rest to me. I will sit in the back." Jason climbed in the back of George's black Rover, which was unmarked. There was no reason to suspect it was a police vehicle.

When they approached the gate, Jason rolled down his window. The guard, a small Chinese man, approached. Another much older guard looked down at them through the glass windows of the gatehouse.

"I'm Jason Steed. I work for Lin Cho. I have some urgent news for Boudica."

"Who's this man?" asked the guard pointing a nicotine-stained finger.

"Oh, that's just George. He's my driver."

"Boudica is not here. You will have to come back later."

"No, it's urgent," Jason said as he stepped out of the car. "We will have to call her from the guardhouse." He walked into the guardhouse to ensure the guard inside didn't raised the alarm.

Jason strolled in and spoke to the guard, who was drinking a mug of tea and working on a newspaper crossword puzzle. Jason was not proud of what he was about to do, but thinking about Kinver and how he was suffering made it easier.

"I need to call Boudica. It's urgent," Jason said. The old guard smiled at Jason—so young and innocent looking. He briefly took his eyes off the boy while he lifted the phone receiver. Jason hopped on his right foot and gave a hard kick with his left foot, hitting the guard in the chest and knocking him back against the wall. The guard fell to the floor, winded. Jason threw a second kick that landed across the guard's face. The guard's head smashed back against the wall. He slowly slid down the wall into an unconscious heap.

George appeared with the second guard in a headlock. He used his other hand to call on the radio. Within a few seconds, two uniformed police officers took the man. George ran to his car with Jason in tow. He sped through the gates to the warehouse where Kinver was being held.

The morning silence was broken by the sound of police sirens as blue-and-white police cars sped into the compound. The guards with the dogs patrolling the perimeter released them in a bid to escape.

George and Jason simultaneously jumped out of his Rover and tried the door on the factory. It was locked. George took a step back and ran at it, hitting it hard with his shoulder. The door lock gave, and the door flew open. George ran inside, quickly followed by Jason, who ran passed him down a corridor. As he turned a corner, they came into a large open area. Two guards shouted at Jason and ran toward him. A third guard shouted from behind them and also gave chase.

Jason felt adrenaline rush through his body. His first karate instructor, Wong Tong, had shown him how to use an adrenaline rush as a powerful weapon. He had explained that when a mother saw her child run over by a car, she had the strength to lift the car or how a man in a field being chased by a bull had enough adrenaline to leap and clear a fence. Jason could force it through his body, triggering full alertness. The only disadvantage was that afterward, he would be very tired. Adrenaline burned the body's sugar levels.

The closest guard tried to grab Jason. Jason ducked and dove to the floor in a push-up position and swung his legs around, knocking the man's own legs away and bringing him down to the floor. Jason sprang to his feet and threw a full roundhouse kick at the second guard, catching him in the chest. Jason leapt in the air and landed with full force on his right foot against the man's knee. The result, as intended, shattered the man's kneecap. He screamed in pain and rolled around on the floor, holding his knee. The first guard was now back up on his feet. He dove at Jason with outstretched arms. Jason jumped back and then kicked out with his right foot—directly into the guard's face. The impact made a crack as the guard's nose broke, and pain shot through his body. He fell to the ground, blood gushing from his nose.

"Stitch that!" George shouted as he head-butted the guard that approached from behind. Jason looked up to see the guard falling backward, blood already streaming from his nose. Jason gave George a smile and nod of approval before he headed off down a corridor. He found the room where he had last seen Kinver and burst through the doors. Kinver was still on the bed. Jason went over to him to wake him and grabbed his arm. It was cold and stiff. He pulled away and cringed. Kinver was dead.

"Is he okay?" George asked, panting as he entered the room.

"No, we're too late. Look, they have burned his chest with something." Jason grimaced as he pointed at fresh burn marks on Jim's chest. Another guard had come up behind George and put his arm around his throat and pulled George back. They fell on the ground, with George desperately trying to get a hand on his attacker. Jason started to run over to help; however, a side door opened and two identical men in white coats appeared.

Wing and Wong. I wondered where you would be, Jason said to himself. One of them ran at Jason, screaming as he approached. He leapt in the air and aimed a high kick toward Jason's face. Jason jumped aside and retaliated with a kick of his own. It was blocked by the man's forearm. He spun around to kick Jason.

So we know karate, do we? What style? I wonder. Jason said to himself.

Jason defended himself, blocking blow after blow from his attacker. He didn't attempt to attack back. He was trying to size up his opponent. George was still struggling with the guard on the floor.

Tae kwon do—good style and fast.

Now that Jason knew what he was up against, he launched an attack on Wing, kicking out in succession, jumping from foot to foot. Wong joined in. The fight began in earnest. Grunts of pain and effort, showers of sweat, and smears of blood covered Jason. No doubt Jason was fast—his punches and kicks powerful and precise. He delivered as good as he got, but he was facing two very determined martial arts experts. When Jason drove Wong to his knees, Wing took his place so there was always one of them fighting him while the other got a breath.

They clearly hoped to wear Jason down. Bloody and bruised, they continued their relentless assault until Jason drove his fingers into the windpipe of one of his assailants and crushed the man's trachea. As Wong staggered back and fell to the ground, gasping and snorting like a pig, Wing's attention slipped for a second. Jason was high on adrenaline. His gift of quick reflexes, along with years of training, made a lethal combination, and he recoiled his right leg. The savage kick caught Wing off-guard—the blow breaking his jaw in two places. Doctors would later have to fit three titanium plates to get his jaw back together.

Jason leapt over Wing and threw a roundhouse kick at the other twin, who was trying to get to his feet. Wong fell and landed on his back. Jason pounced on him with his knee in the man's chest, followed by more than a dozen punches into Wong's blood-covered face. He heard George gasping for air from his attacker, who still had his arms around his throat.

Jason cursed and ran to George's aid. He kicked out at the man's face, breaking the man's nose and rendering him unconscious. Jason stepped over George, who was rubbing his throat and trying to get to his feet. Jason attacked the unconscious man again. George watched as Jason dived at the man, who was already not moving. Jason turned him over and pounded the man's face with an onslaught of fast, well-aimed punches. Blood splattered back into Jason's face and mixed with his own blood and sweat. He panted heavily as he tried to gasp for oxygen to supply his lungs.

"Jason, stop. He isn't going anywhere," George said.

The pounding continued.

"Jason, stop," George shouted. "I think you bloody killed him—stop!" Jason, who seemed to lose control, becoming a brutal and savage predator, shocked George.

Jason then stopped and sat on the floor next to his blood-covered prey. He panted heavily. Sweat and blood rained down his face. He wiped his face with his trembling hands. Several police officers ran into the room. George took control. They called an ambulance to collect the wounded. They were visibly stunned by the sight of Jason's victims.

"Look, sir," a young officer who was holding up a clipboard with writing on it said. "It looks like they got Kinver to talk."

"What does it say?" George asked, still rubbing his throat. The SYUI officer walked over.

"It's in Chinese, but it has two names written in English on it," he said, showing his superior. George took it and walked over to Jason. He still sat on the floor, his elbows resting on his knees, his head down. George kneeled down beside him.

"Are you all right, Jason?" George asked sympathetically.

Jason looked up, his nose still running with blood and his hair and face covered in blood splashes. Jason looked at the back of his trembling hands. His knuckles were split open. They were also covered in his and his victim's blood.

"Tired, sir."

"You speak Chinese. What does this say? It looks like they got poor Jim Kinver to speak after all."

Jason glanced at it. "It says George Young and Jason Steed. The rest is in Chinese."

"I bloody know that, don't I? What does the Chinese say?" George shouted impatiently. His sympathetic feelings did not last long.

"I can speak Chinese. I have no idea how to read it." Jason bowed his head back down. He was still trembling.

Boudica's men had started a fire to try to burn the evidence. The wooden pallets and boxes burned rapidly, and a hungry blaze raged through the building. Smoke started to fill the corridors.

A police officer pulled Jason to his feet. They had to get out of the blazing inferno.

CHAPTER 11

MRS. BRISTOW GENTLY WOKE Janice by giving her a kiss on the cheek.

"Morning, sweetheart. It's time to get up," she said, picking up Janice's clothes from yesterday off the carpet. "Oh, and if you want to spend half an hour in the bathroom getting ready, at least wait until Jason has used the toilet. Yesterday, the poor boy stood outside dancing on the spot." She headed into Jason's room.

Oh, no, Jason. How am I going to explain that? Maybe the police brought him back after the doctor and Scott dropped me off, Janice thought, dreading what might happen if he was still out.

"Jason," Mrs. Bristow shouted as she ran out of his room. "Jason…he's gone!" Mr. Bristow came out of the kitchen and helped look for him. It was not long before they came into Janice's room to look for him.

"He's not here. He's at the police station. He's been there all night," Janice admitted.

"What has he done now?" her father asked. "Why didn't you tell us?"

Janice tried to explain, but she was cut off by the doorbell. Thinking it might be Jason and she'd be off the hook, Janice jumped up to get it.

"I have a package for Mr. and Mrs. Bristow," a man said. He was wearing black leather motorcycle trousers and a jacket.

He wore a large, black, full-face crash helmet. Janice took the package and went into the kitchen, where her parents were starting breakfast.

"It's a delivery for you," Janice said as she handed the package to her mother. Mrs. Bristow looked puzzled and started to open the parcel.

The explosion could be heard from miles around. Not a single window was left intact. Glass and debris showered the few parked cars below the apartments. The explosion also blew a hole in the ceiling, damaging the apartment upstairs and killing the cat. The fire that burned afterward completely gutted the apartment. The bodies of the Bristow family were never found.

CHAPTER 12

WHEN JASON EMERGED FROM Boudica's blazing factory, he was faced with a parking lot full of flashing sirens from police cars, ambulances, and fire trucks. He staggered toward George's car, coughing from the smoke. He needed to sleep somewhere. He limped a few paces when two paramedics swiftly approached him. They walked him to the ambulance and told him to lie on the bed while they cleaned the blood from his hands and face. His nose had finally stopped bleeding. The loss of blood and earlier exertion had drained Jason's young body of all his energy.

"You'll be all right now, son. I'll take you to St. Mary's Hospital and they will check you over," the paramedic said.

"No, I want to go home now," Jason coughed. Jason climbed off the bed and tried to stand. The paramedic pushed against Jason's shoulder.

"No, son, stay on the bed. You need to go to the hospital. You are injured and have breathed in a lot of smoke."

Jason swiftly knocked his hand away. "I'm not in the mood to argue, sir. I want to go home. I need to see George Young." Jason stood. He could just see George talking to some other officers. George caught sight of Jason standing in the doorway of the ambulance and broke away to talk to him.

"You all right, son?" George asked.

"I want to go home, George. I'm okay. I don't need the hospital." George studied Jason. He looked so small. His normally shiny blond hair was matted with blood and dried sweat. His face was still covered with soot, and his hands were covered in fresh bandages. George felt guilty for using such a young boy on an operation. He has a fifteen-year-old son of his own and would never dream of putting him through this.

"You're right, son. I will drive you myself. That's the least I can do." He put his arm on Jason's shoulder and led the boy to his car. The drive home started quiet. Jason sat heavily in the front seat, fighting to stay awake. His and George's eyes were still stinging from the smoke.

"Jason, if you don't mind me saying, you lost it back there, didn't you?"

Jason didn't reply.

"You just kept hitting that guy. It was bloody scary to watch you like that."

Jason sighed. "I build up adrenalin in my body and use it as a weapon. It helps me fight. Without it, I could never take on those twins and win. I just can't control it properly yet. It's worse when I lose my temper."

There was a long silence.

"I wanted to thank you, Jason, not just back there for getting that guy off me but for the whole operation. Oh, and I'll need you to make a statement regarding the murder of Russell Watson. They'll arrest Andrew Cho for that and the store owner's murder." Jason's eyes had closed, but at George's statement, they popped opened.

"What did you say? Store owner?" Jason looked horrified. George looked away from Jason's glare and kept his eyes on the road. "It was a real knife? You tricked me! I killed him." Jason punched his own forehead with the back of his hand and swore at George.

"Come on, Jason. We couldn't use a fake knife. Cho may have noticed and the whole bleeding operation would have been at risk."

Another long silence.

Jason stared out the window and said quietly, "I will never forgive you for doing this."

After an awkward silence, George turned on his police radio. The voice over the radio was giving details about a large explosion at an apartment block. It was suspected to be a gas pipe accident.

CHAPTER 13

AFTER JUST THREE HOURS of sleep, Jason was woken by angry shouting downstairs in the hallway. At first, he thought he was dreaming, but it returned and alerted him. Someone with a deep Scottish accent shouted, "No, out of the question. Over my dead body."

Jason recognized the voice of his grandfather. Jason still felt guilty after the talk he had had with his grandfather when he had gotten home. He told Jason that he had worried his grandmother sick and that he was disappointed in him. Jason protested that he was undercover and couldn't tell his grandparents what was happening, but he realized that he had never stopped to think how they might have felt. He leapt out of bed and hurried to the top of the stairs so he could see what was happening.

George was at the front door. His grandfather was blocking the entrance—his grandmother at his side. Mrs. Beeton was on the phone, talking to someone. She also looked agitated.

"It's too bloody important to argue about. I need to see Jason. Either you move or I'll move you," George shouted, pointing his finger in Jason's grandfather's face. Jason was walking barefoot down the wooden staircase. He jumped down the last four steps and ran up to the door.

"You lay a finger on my grandparents and I break every bone in your body. What do you want now?" Jason shouted. He stepped between his grandfather and George. His grandfather rested his hands on Jason's shoulders and lovingly stroked the back of Jason's neck with his thumbs while George explained.

"Jason, the gas explosion at the apartment block? It turns out that was no accident. It was a bomb. It was the Bristows' home."

"Oh…are they hurt?" Jason asked, concerned.

"They didn't stand a chance, son. The place is gutted. I'm sorry. My home was also attacked with a mortar. It blew the bloody roof off. Jean and my son were staying at her mother's, thank God. Jean and I aren't getting on too good. You know, grown-up stuff. Anyway, bloody lucky really."

Jason could see the fear in George's eyes. The man's hands were shaking, and he looked very frightened. Two armed police officers stood on the doorstep with him, and Jason wondered if they were bodyguards. He was devastated to hear what had happened to the Bristow family.

"Dr. Turner is coming over," Mrs. Beeton said. "I told him we were having trouble with *you*," she said, glaring at George. She stood next to Jason's gran—the three of them standing together behind Jason.

"What do you want with me?" Jason asked.

"It's not safe, Jason. If Boudica works out you live here, they will come after you."

"They? We caught them. You should have them locked up."

"Boudica has not been seen and the Chos have also disappeared. Once they got Jim Kinver to talk, they went into hiding. Our information is that Boudica has a large bounty on me and my family, the Lin Tse-Hsu family, and you, Jason."

"Who is Lin Tse-Hsu?" Jason asked.

"Lin Tse-Hsu is the Chinese commissioner and a supporter of Chairman Mao. He is working hard to stop corruption in China and has frozen all of Boudica's Chinese assets. Our informants believe Boudica will try to snatch someone he cares about so she can ransom the release of her funds. His youngest daughter attends school here just outside London. We believe that she is a target."

What George didn't say—and couldn't prove—was that he suspected the Triads had been tipped off. The Cho family had fled their home just minutes before the raid.

"What have you done? What have you gotten him into? He is just a wee schoolboy. He came home covered in blood with his hands in bandages and his body covered in bruises. Why can't you leave the boy alone?" Mrs. Macintosh scolded.

"Sir, a car is approaching," one of the armed police officers warned.

Jason looked out the open door.

"That's Scott and his father," Jason said before he squeezed out the door past George. Before the car stopped, Scott was opening the car door. He jumped out and ran up to Jason. They gave a brief welcome hug, and Dr. Turner ruffled Jason's hair.

"Is everything all right, Jason? Mrs. Beeton called and asked for help," Dr. Turner said.

"I'll let them explain. I'd better get dressed." Jason went up to his room with Scott to get dressed. It felt good to get into his own clothes at last. For weeks, he had been wearing the juvic overalls or the clothes Mrs. Bristow had bought him.

"Jason, what's with the bandages?" Scott asked.

"I cut my knuckles up pretty bad. I had some good fights

though. Unfortunately, Jim Kinver was already dead, and he'd talked. Help me with my buttons and belt. I can't do it with these bandages," Jason said, trying to do his shirt up.

As Jason and Scott came thundering back down the stairs, George was suggesting that the Macintoshes go back up to Scotland.

"Then Jason will be coming with us. We'll take him to Scotland," Jason Macintosh demanded.

"No, Mrs. Macintosh, that won't be safe. If these geezers work out where he lives and come here, they might find something to trace him back to you. We can't protect him in Scotland," George argued.

"I can ask to stay with Princess Catherine at Buckingham Palace. They have great security," Jason suggested.

"No, we can't put the Queen at risk, Jason. I've already made plans. You're flying to Spain this afternoon," George said. "Pack a bag. You won't need much—it'll be hot. Treat it like a vacation paid for by Her Majesty's government for all your help."

"Do I have to? I have just got back home! I've missed tons of school and I haven't spoken to Catherine for weeks. That's not fair," Jason whined, showing his age. He was acting like any normal boy who didn't get his own way.

"Will Scott be safe?" Dr. Turner asked.

"I believe so. He's pretty smart, that one. Used a fake name when he went to visit Jason, so they can't trace him. However, I will be placing a police guard outside your home twenty-four hours a day. It's just to be on the safe side."

Within ten minutes, Jason was once again saying good-bye to his family and friends.

CHAPTER 14

You'll be traveling with my family and Lin Tse-Hsu's daughter, Joanne. I told the 'Trouble and Strife' that she's helping hide two children—nothing more. My boy isn't too happy about two strange kids coming along, but he'll have to make do. I got a villa up in the mountains in Spain just north of Malaga. It's got a swimming pool, and you will get to have a well-needed rest. But most importantly, it's safe. It's the last place in the world anyone would suspect. You'll hide out until we capture Boudica."

"And what about you, George?" Jason asked.

"I got myself into this mess. I will get meself out. I will catch Boudica and the Chos. I'll make them bleeding pay for all this hassle."

They drove for nearly an hour toward Kent and turned down a tree-lined road. Jason read the sign: "Benedon Girls School."

"This is Catherine's school. I've been here before." He grinned.

"Looks like a right stuck-up school," George grunted. "I bet the kids who go here don't even fart."

Benedon School thrust into the air proudly—the main building towering imposingly over the smaller wings. The entrance was flung wide open as if with greeting. George marveled.

The car slowed down as it drove into the front courtyard. The two-hundred-year-old building stood majestically before them. A group of girls stood in the doorway and talked. Jason opened his door and jumped out. One of the girls had a suitcase with her. She was Asian and about eleven years old. George smiled as he climbed out and opened his trunk, thinking Jason was going to collect the girl's case. Jason walked passed her, his eyes looking farther back at two girls talking.

"We have to stop meeting like this." He grinned at the two girls.

"Jason!" Catherine screamed with a huge smile. "What a nice surprise." She dropped her books and threw her arms around him.

George shook his head and paced toward them. A lady with glasses balanced on the end of her nose came out of the corridor and coughed behind Catherine and Jason, who were now hugging and rubbing foreheads.

"Miss Catherine, you do know the rules about boys and safety. We can't have strangers turning up whenever they feel like it," she said abruptly.

George introduced himself and showed his ID. Mrs. Cookson, the school principal, shook his hand and introduced George to Miss Tse-Hsu.

Joanne Tse-Hsu slightly bowed her head as she shook George's hand. She smiled nervously at him. Her left hand was playing with one of the pigtails that hung down her chest.

"Is that *boy* with you, Mr. Young?" Mrs. Cookson asked as she jabbed a finger at Jason, who was still hugging Catherine.

"Yeah, that's Jason. He's coming with us," George said, trying to conceal a smirk.

"Well, I hope he keeps his hands off Miss Tse-Hsu," she tutted.

"Jason, we have to go. Put her down," George shouted with a grin on his face.

Jason quickly explained to Catherine that he had to go away and could not say where. He said he and Joanne were being taken to a safe house. The meeting was very brief, but he was glad he had a chance to see her at last. He realized how much he had missed her. He gave a tight-lip smile to Joanne. They gave a nod but didn't speak. She had no idea who he was or how he knew Princess Catherine. Joanne looked just as unhappy as Jason about the situation.

George tried to make conversation on the drive back into the city, but his attempts fell on deaf ears. Joanne gazed out the car window as she sucked on her hair. She was good-looking with large, dark eyes and black hair tied in two long pigtails. Jason looked at her through his long blond bangs, which hung over his eyes. The rest of his hair was short, but he kept the front as long as he could. He had done this since he had been old enough to argue about his haircuts. He was naturally shy and had always felt safe behind his bangs.

George stopped outside a home in a quiet suburb of London. Large chestnut trees shaded the front gardens. The redbrick, terraced home was surrounded by rose bushes and flowering red geraniums.

George disappeared into the house. A while later, the Young family came out with suitcases. George placed their luggage in the trunk and introduced Jason and Joanne to his family.

"Right then. This is the boy I told you about—Jason. He's quiet and no trouble. I am sure you will all get along. Martin, Jason's a good swimmer. You boys will have a good time. And this is Jong Tse-Hsu...or Joanne, as she calls herself here."

Martin, George's fifteen-year-old son, looked down at Jason. He had jet-black hair like his father and was a little overweight, with acne spread around his mouth. He sat in the back of the car and ignored the rest of them, flipping through a football magazine.

"Hello, pet. I'm Mrs. Young. You can call me Jean," Mrs. Young said, shaking Jason's hand gently. Jason forced a smile. "What did you do to your hands?"

"I fell on some broken glass." He looked up at George after he lied. George gave an agreeing nod. His wife and son did not need to know everything.

At the airport, George kissed his family good-bye at the departure gates and took Jason to one side.

"Jason, I ain't been that honest with you," George said, looking Jason in the eye.

"So what's new?" Jason shrugged.

"Yeah, I guess I deserve that. Look, I had a tough job getting the higher-ups to let you go so Spain. SYUI wanted to keep you and Joanne locked up safe. I know a couple kids don't want to be stuck in a safe house, so I got you this. Plus, I have the other benefit."

"What other benefit?" Jason asked.

"I know you will look after my family, Jason. You will all be safe, but just in case, please look after them," George said, holding out his hand.

"I will. Besides, Joanne is kinda cute," Jason said, winking and grinning. George returned the grin and nodded.

CHAPTER 15

JEAN SAT IN A row of three seats with Martin and Joanne. Jason had to sit next to a red-haired man and his three-year-old daughter, who insisted on sitting by the window and then using the bathroom every ten minutes. The two-hour flight seemed endless to Jason. Although, Jason could have sworn that an Asian man sitting several rows away kept looking at him. *I'm probably just being paranoid.*

At Malaga Airport, Jean rented a lime-green Volkswagen Beetle. The little car had no air-conditioning. As the car twisted its way up the narrow mountain roads, the temperature inside became unbearable. They eventually arrived at Villa Rosa—high in the Spanish mountains. It was just off the main road down a small dirt track. The white building with a terra-cotta roof stood out on a ledge overlooking some of Spain's finest scenery. Just below Villa Rosa was another similar villa owned by a French writer and his young wife.

Villa Rosa had a pool on the terrace surrounded by a grape-vine. George and Jean had used the villa for many holidays. Martin was upset when he found out he had to share his room with Jason and insisted on calling him "that boy" despite Jean's attempts to chastise him.

Back in the United Kingdom, SYUI raided several properties owned by members of the Triads. Many were arrested on small theft charges or tax evasion—any charges the police could come up with. However, none of them would give up any information on Boudica.

Every shop and supermarket had to remove Coco-Bites from its shelves. Many children and some adults throughout the country had major withdrawal symptoms. Boudica's assets were seized, and the Inland Revenue was amazed by how much money she had made in such a short while.

Boudica and Lin Cho had gone underground, and the police were no closer to arresting them despite several failed assassination attempts on Lin Tse-Hsu's life. But in West London, an Asian man and his sumo-sized bodyguard quietly slipped into the back room of a club.

Dark smoke filled the room and stung Cho's eyes as he tried to focus. Boudica sat in a throne-shaped chair. She wore a black, skin-tight, silk shirt and tight black trousers. On the floor next to her eating small cubes of meat out of her hand was a fully grown male leopard. Three other men sat in chairs around the room. A few heads nodded, but none spoke.

"Boudica, it's good to see you again," Cho said, bowing his head nervously.

"Ah, Lin Cho, the very man I wanted to see. You haven't met Luke, have you? He is hungry. Take some meat from the bucket behind you and show him you are a friend," she ordered. Lin dipped his hand into the bucket of warm blood and pulled out some flesh. He slowly approached Luke with his hand outstretched. The leopard lazily stood and opened its huge mouth to reveal large white incisors. As it got close to Lin's hand, it snapped, took the meat, and growled loudly as it chewed. Boudica smiled and clapped her hands in delight.

"More. Give him more. He likes you," she said. Her whole face lit up with excitement. Reluctantly, Lin continued to feed Luke by hand.

Boudica continued to watch, but the smile slid from her face. She glanced at Kotang in the corner before narrowing her eyes on Lin. "My whole operation has been destroyed. I am an embarrassment to our homeland. Everything I have worked for is gone. Do you believe in 'an eye for an eye,' Lin Cho?" Boudica asked.

"Yes, Boudica. This very moment, I have all my men looking for the SYUI man, George Young, and his family. I will personally see to it that they all die. I will bring you the head of George Young," Cho said, his hand dripping with blood from the meat he was feeding the leopard.

"Was it not your son, Andrew, who allowed the 'boy,' Jason Steed, into our operation? You even brought him to my factory yourself! You got careless and allowed a spy among us."

"Boudica, we didn't know! How would we? We checked him out and he was just a boy. Anyway, he's dead. We blew up his home and entire family!"

"His is not the only family about to be destroyed. Andrew is not missing—your mistake has already cost you a son," Boudica said coldly. Lin's face turned gray and he shook his head in disbelief.

"And now…Kotang, they tell me that you can crush a man to death. If you want to work for me now, you will have to prove your worth. Show me how you can crush a man to death," Boudica ordered.

Kotang grabbed Cho from behind, took a deep breath, and started to squeeze.

Back in Spain, the Young family and Jason prepared to go out for the evening.

"How much of that stuff did you put on? It stinks." Jason laughed, waving his hand in front of his nose.

"Not too much. There'll be a disco at the bar and probably some girls. I want to look my best," Martin said. He was standing in his underwear in front of the mirror, arranging his hair. He had covered his neck and chest with aftershave. "Do you want some?" Martin asked, passing the bottle of Hai Karate aftershave. Jason was drying himself off after his shower and examining himself. He was sunburned on his neck, back, and arms.

"No way! I mean, it'll sting my sunburn."

"Ha! So!" Martin shouted as he made a karate move toward Jason. Jason ignored him. "I might take up karate. I would be good at it." He grinned as he threw his arms around in the air.

"You should. It's the best sport you can do," Jason enthused.

It was an hour's drive to Port Malaga. The ancient Spanish town sat in the center of Costa del Sol. Soft sea breezes from the Mediterranean coastline regulated the summer heat, making the harbor a favorite tourist destination for northern Europeans. The ancient streets were overcrowded with modern, oversized hotels, restaurants, and bars. Gift shops selling tacky tourists trinkets of Spanish bullfights, donkeys, and beach towels littered the streets. The ice cream shops had customers spilling onto the payments and out into the busy street. The entire town was relaxed with a party atmosphere.

Jean found a place to park, and they walked along the shops and bars like any other family on vacation. Most of the British and German tourists were sunburned and smelling of coconut oil and mosquito repellent. Jason was relaxed. He enjoyed the company of the others. Jean treated him and Joanne as part of the family, and he was enjoying the motherly attention. Martin was four years older but immature for his age. He made Jason laugh and forget his troubles. Joanne didn't speak much, and when he caught her looking at him, she immediately looked away.

Night was coming, proclaimed by a blinding orange sun piercing an immense, fluffy wall of clouds to the west. Soon darkness would spread across the sky—but not here. Here the blazing neon lights would garnish the harbor and tiny streets.

"This is it. The Red Bull, they cook proper English food and have a disco, so you kids can dance after," Jean explained, tugging Joanne behind her. Jason allowed Martin to follow next. He was about to follow them in when he noticed a man across the street watching them. As soon as Jason glanced his way, the man pretended to be looking at a rack of postcards.

What is he doing on his own? Why is he watching us?

Jason was now concerned. He couldn't be sure, but he could have sworn the guy was the same man he had seen on the airplane.

CHAPTER 16

"Come on, Jason. We are waiting for you," Joanne murmured, grabbing Jason's hand and pulling him inside. She led him to the table where Jean and Martin were smiling broadly at them. Jason then realized Joanne was still holding his hand. He immediately let go and started to blush. He was worried about the man by the postcards, but he told himself that it was just his imagination. What he didn't see was the man on the Vespa scooter taking picture after picture of the happy group.

"Looks like you've already found yourself a girl, Jason," Martin said and grinned, knocking Jason with his elbow.

Joanne beamed. Her large dark eyes sparkled.

"I'll have whatever Jason is having," Joanne said as she moved her chair closer to his.

Distracted and still a little rattled, Jason retorted angrily. "Order your own stuff and don't hold my hand again. I already have a girlfriend," he barked above the noise of the music.

When the waitress brought them their food, she asked if Joanne was all right. She noticed her face was red and tears were running down her cheeks. Jason felt guilty and was quiet until they got back to the villa.

Everyone quietly drifted off to different parts of the villa and went to bed. Jason was just about to turn over when Martin pounced on his bed, pinned him down, and glared into Jason's face, his nose touching Jason's.

"You upset that Joanne again, and I'll give you a black eye, karate or no karate. You got that?" Martin hissed at Jason, spitting into his face at the same time. Jason thought about throwing him off and hitting him, but Martin was just trying to be protective. It was a noble thing to do.

"Okay. I'm sorry. I'll apologize to her in the morning. Get off me."

"Good," Martin said, pushing himself up off of Jason. "Next time, you won't get a warning."

Jason turned over. He wished it was over and he was lying in his own bed or getting ready for school at St. Joseph's. He wished he was eating Mrs. Beeton's fabulous cooking and carrot cake and seeing his friends, Scott and Catherine.

Catherine—

With that thought, he fell asleep.

The next two days were uneventful. Joanne kept her distance from Jason and stayed close to Jean. Martin seemed to spend a lot of time alone on a lower lawn that overlooked the villa below. Jason spent hours in the pool, swimming length after length. When he warmed up, he pulled himself out of the pool and practiced his karate katas.

"Jean, why are boys so weird? Martin spends all day on the lawn by himself looking out at sea with the binoculars, and

Jason swims nonstop for an hour and then spends hours doing those stupid karate movements. I hate karate. My father and my brothers do it, as it's our tradition, but not me," Joanne whined.

"Keeah," Jason shouted as he made a strike forward. He moved on the balls of his feet and toes with precision, speed, and grace. Sweat trickled down his chest and dried in the strong sun.

They watched Jason as he gracefully moved across the pool deck with a variety of karate stances and moves.

"He seems like a nice boy. We can go into town again tonight and try a different restaurant."

"Yeah, and I won't make the mistake of holding Jason's hand." She paused and grinned. "Although he did apologize for that, but I've still not forgiven him. I hope he feels bad."

Jason went inside and came out of the villa carrying two glasses of water. He smiled at Jean and Joanne. Jean smiled back, but Joanne looked away with her nose raised. He walked down to the lower lawn, where Martin was lying on his stomach and looking over the edge. He had been here for a few hours. Jason wanted to talk to someone, so he thought it was time he made up with Martin.

"I thought you might want a cold drink. It's hot out here," Jason said as he approached.

"Shhh. Keep your voice down," Martin snapped back, grinning like the Cheshire Cat. He sat up and took the glass of water and then said, "Thanks." He drank the water down without stopping, wiped his mouth, and burped. "Can you keep a secret?" he asked, grinning.

"Sure can," Jason said, grinning back and sitting down next to him.

"Look down there." Martin pointed down on the villa below. Jason lay on his stomach and looked. A woman was sunbathing naked next to the pool. She was lying on her back and revealing her body.

"You dirty old man," Jason whispered. "So this is what you have been looking at." Jason turned and grinned at Martin. Martin lay down next to him, both boys watching.

"I don't think this is right," Jason whispered.

"Then go back to the pool, but don't say anything to my mum. I'm staying here."

Jason started to lift himself up to go back, but curiosity was getting the better of him, even though he knew it was wrong.

"Do you think she would let me rub some sunscreen on her?" Martin joked, gesturing with his hands on his own chest.

Jason had to put his hand over his mouth to stop himself from laughing out loud. Suddenly a loud scream came from behind them up at the villa. It was so loud that the sunbathing lady also heard it and looked up. She caught both boys watching her. Immediately, Jason jumped back, his face flushed bright red with embarrassment.

"She saw us! She'll think we're perverts or something. It's all your fault," Jason said, completely flustered.

Martin lay on his back, laughing at Jason. "If she doesn't like it, she should cover up."

"Come on. We'd better check what that scream was about."

As they walked back up toward the villa, Martin teased Jason, whose face was still bright. They were still laughing as they walked into the villa.

Just inside the door, Martin felt a cold metal object shoved against his head. Jason turned to face the threat, but it was too late.

CHAPTER 17

A SECOND MAN APPEARED AND held Jason at gunpoint. They were taken into Jean's bedroom. She was sitting on the bed and crying. Her hair was a mess, and she had a cut just below her left eye. Joanne was hugging her and sobbing. Two more gunmen were in the room, smiling at the boys. They were all wearing black T-shirts and tight black pants. All four men were Chinese and in their midtwenties. Jason could not be sure, but one looked like the man he had seen in Malaga.

"I don't like to kill children, but I have a job to do. Your husband has caused our boss many problems. So now his family will die. The girl comes with us," a gunman coldly said. Martin climbed onto the bed and hugged his mother.

"What about this boy?" asked a shorter man with a scar on his face, pointing at Jason.

"He wasn't part of the job, but he could call the cops before we get clear." The man looked at Jason, trying to decide what to do with the boy.

"Tie me up and gag me, sir. Make sure I can't get free for hours and hours. You'll be far away with Joanne by the time someone finds me," Jason said. He then crouched down and held out his hands in a begging position. "Please, sir. Don't hurt me." He started a fake cry. As far as Boudica was concerned, Jason had been killed in the bomb at the Bristows' apartment.

"Very well. Get something to tie up the boy with," he ordered. One of the men left to find some rope. "You see, I have a heart. It's just business. Now who wants to go first? Mother?"

Joanne clung tight to Jean. Jason caught Joanne glaring at him with hate in her eyes. She was now convinced he was a coward.

"I found a rope. I can tie him to the stove. Boy, come with me," said the returning gunman. Jason followed him to the kitchen. Once next to the stove, Jason put his hands together, ready to be tied up. The gunman set his gun on top of the stove and moved toward Jason.

The move was so fast the gunman saw just a blur. Jason grabbed the man's shirt with his left hand and pulled him toward him. At the same time, Jason threw a full-fisted punch, using everything he had. When his fist was inches from connecting, Jason also threw his shoulder into the blow to increase the power. It struck the man's windpipe, completely shattering it. He collapsed onto the kitchen floor and held his throat. Jason grabbed the kitchen towel and dove down on the man. He forced the towel against the man's mouth so his gasping sounds could not be heard. After just over a minute, the man's wriggling body went limp.

Not wanting to waste a second, Jason picked up the gun and ran back toward the bedroom. The leader had his gun aimed at the bed. Jason sprinted toward the door, aimed, and fired, shooting the gunman in the shoulder and knocking him down. Jean and Joanne screamed. The loud bang and recoil of the gun also gave Jason a scare. He had shot a gun before, but he was still surprised by how loud it was.

Jason ran through the door, twisted his body, and aimed the

gun at the man behind the wall. Before the man could raise his gun, Jason shot him twice. The first bullet hit him in the neck, but the second missed and buried itself in the wall. Jason kept his momentum going and leapt onto the bed. He landed on his right leg and then he bounced and kicked out with his left at the fourth gunman, catching the man in his chest.

The gunman was thrown back against the wall. He was stunned but still standing, and worse still, he held onto his gun. Jason landed next to him on the floor and struck out at the hand with the gun. It fired and sent a bullet into the ceiling.

With his other hand, the gunman grabbed for Jason's weapon. He wrapped his hand around Jason's, which was still gripping the gun he'd gotten off the guy in the kitchen, and tried to turn it on Jason. Overpowered by the man's stronger hands, Jason brought his knee up into the man's groin. The gunman screamed out and fell to his knees, taking Jason with him. But the man still clung to both guns.

"Help me," Jason shouted to Martin. He was now pinned down and was slowly losing the grip on his gun. No help came. The others huddled together, terrified. Jason tried a judo throw. He was used to training with adults and hoped he could use the man's weight advantage against him. It worked, and the man went over Jason's shoulders. He landed on his back but didn't let go of the guns.

But Jason saw the barrel of the gun was now covered by the man's hand, so he pulled the trigger. Blood splattered both of them, and the man let go of both guns and clenched his hand while he cursed and screamed in pain. A bullet to the head silenced him. Jason got up and kneeled down next to the leader, who was lying on the ground and holding his shoulder. Jason stuck the gun under the wounded man's chin.

"Who sent you?" Jason shouted. Before he could answer, a bullet zinged past Jason. A fifth gunman entered and shot at Jason again, but he had missed and hit his own man. Jason dove behind the bed. He looked under it and could see a man creeping forward. He shot his last two bullets into the man's foot and ankle. The gunman screamed in pain and crashed to the ground. Jason was up and over the bed. He picked up the man's gun, kneeled down, and asked the same question.

"Okay, since you killed him, I'll ask you. Who sent you?" Jason shouted after he stuck the gun under the man's chin.

"I don't speak English," the man said back in Chinese. He was in severe pain. Sweat beads started to form on his face.

Jason asked again, this time in Chinese, "Who sent you? If you don't tell me, I will shoot." The Youngs and Joanne looked at Jason in amazement. Not only could he shoot and fight, he could also speak Chinese.

"Boudica."

"How many others are there?" Jason asked, pushing the gun harder against the man.

"Three." With that answer, Jason pulled back his gun. With his right hand, he squeezed the man's main artery to the brain. Within a few seconds, the man was unconscious.

"Come on. We have to get out of here," Jason said as he picked up another gun. "Come on…move. There's another three hit men, and they will stop at nothing until you two are dead."

Jason crept to the front door. He could see two cars farther up the drive. Alongside them, there stood three men watching the villa. Jason ran back into the bedroom, where the others were still sitting on the bed and sobbing.

"Mrs. Young, we are going out the window. We will climb down to the next villa and try to get help."

With tears running down her face, she nodded back. Jason went first and the others followed. They crept down to the lower lawn and started to climb down the bank to the villa below. It was quite steep, and when they got close to the bottom, they found a twelve-foot drop to the patio on the villa below. Jason looked down. He was sure he could jump it but unsure if Mrs. Young and Joanne could. He paused, looking for a better way. Martin caught up with him and jumped down.

"Pass Joanne down to me," he said, raising his arms. He was then knocked across the back of the head with a broomstick.

"*Pervers…aller loin,*" the young woman shouted in French. "*Pervers!*"

Martin crouched down and tried to defend himself. Joanne let out a huge scream. Jason quickly turned and told her to be quiet, but it was now probably too late.

"*Nous avons besoin d'aide. Appelez la police,*" Jason shouted to her in French. The woman looked up at Jason and pointed.

"*Pervers,*" she screamed.

"*Appelez la police,*" Jason shouted back as he lowered Joanne down. The French woman decided to follow Jason's advice and call the police. Jean jumped down herself followed by Jason.

"What was she saying?" Jean asked.

"I don't know. I told her to call the police," Jason lied as he checked to see if they were being followed.

"I thought she called you a—" Jean said only to be interrupted by Martin.

"Well, she *is* French. They're all crazy. Too much wine, snails, and frog legs," Martin said, trying to change the subject and, with rolling eyes, mimicking someone drinking. "Jason, just how many languages do you speak?"

"Run!" Jason shouted. "They're coming."

CHAPTER 18

TWO MEN WERE CLIMBING down the bank, and the other was driving his car along the French owner's driveway toward the villa. They followed Jason behind the villa. The lawn met a grove of orange trees. "Come on. We have to hide."

They followed Jason into the grove. It ran down the side of the mountain. Jason stopped to take his bearings.

"This way," he said, climbing up the steep mountain. "The trees will give us cover."

"No, Jason, we should go down toward Malaga. It will be easier and faster," Jean replied, grabbing Joanne by the hand.

"No!" Jason was defiant.

"Jason, Mum is right. That's too hard-going. None of us have any shoes on, and it's much easier to go down and try to get help," Martin said, walking downward. Two gunshots were heard.

"What was that? Are they shooting at us?" Joanne screamed.

"No, that was probably the French lady getting shot. Look, I know it's easy to go down and quicker, but that is what they would expect. Wong Tong says to win a battle, you must do the opposite to what your enemy expects. We go up," Jason commanded. Reluctantly, they followed Jason, who was running up the steep hillside and keeping close to the thick cover of the orange trees.

After twenty minutes, Jason stopped and sat down cross-legged. The heat was intense, buffeting his face. He examined his feet. The rough terrain of the Spanish mountain was made up of stones, volcanic rock, and dirt. Jason's feet were cut and bleeding. He tried to pull out the tiny stones and sand particles from his cuts. Joanne joined him and checked her feet. She was still sobbing and shaking.

"Jason, just who are you? And who is Wong Tong?" Martin asked, sitting on the ground and panting.

"Wong Tong was my karate instructor in Hong Kong. I was born there and moved to England when I was ten. That's where I learned to speak Chinese."

"But who are you? You just shot all those men and fought them by yourself," Jean said.

"I've got a black belt in various styles of karate and judo. I've been working for George undercover."

"So you are—what? A boy spy?" Martin asked.

"No, I'm—" Jason started but paused. "I don't know what I am. I'm just helping SYUI."

"You killed back there and I don't think this is your first time," Jean said, hugging Joanne.

"I was in Jakarta with the Sea Cadets when we were attacked. I was one of the lucky survivors."

"Oh, that was horrible, you poor boy," Joanne said.

"Okay, I think we should keep going a bit farther. We need to get help," Jason said, standing painfully. They followed him farther up the mountain. The pace was much slower now.

The hot Costa del Sol sun dried the air and burned into Jason's back. He and Martin were wearing just swimming trunks. The terrain got rougher the higher they went until they came to the end of the orange grove. Jason stopped and tried to shelter himself from the sun under one of the last orange trees.

"I can't go on. My feet are burning. The stones are too hot," Martin complained as he sat down next to Jason.

"Jason, I think we should rest," Jean said, wiping the sweat from her face with her forearm. Jason nodded and looked down. His neck and shoulders were badly sunburned. It felt good to take the weight off his feet.

"You're right. I think we should stay here until its gets dark. We'll be in the open once we move forward. It will be much safer to go on under the cover of darkness."

"I'm not staying up here all night." Jean said. "You will have to think of something else."

Jason looked at her incredulously. "Think of something else? What do you think I am?" He said loudly.

"You're a spy. Dad put you with us to look after us." Martin snapped back.

"I'm not a spy. I am here for my protection as much as yours. I don't have a plan or any clue how to get out of this. George asked *you* to look after us," he said gesturing at Joanne.

"Then why did you lead us up here?" Jean said crossly.

"To survive—that's all. To go down would have meant capture and death. Look at me. I have no shoes or shirt. Just a gun stuffed down my swimming shorts. My feet are killing me too. I don't know what to do." The others went quiet and looked at each other. Jason sat back down with his back to them. Jean sat down next to Jason. She could see he was getting upset. She put her hand on Jason's arm.

"Sorry, honey. We don't blame you. We are all just scared. You saved our lives and got us this far. We will work this out together."

The comforting words were emotional for Jason. He looked down to the ground and watched a teardrop land in the gravel below him. He wiped his face and eyes and tried to think of something.

After another three hours, the light faded from the sky and an indigo glow descended on the scenery. The relentless heat of the sun vanished. The air became cool and faintly smelled of the sweet aroma from the orange grove.

They continued on and over the jagged top of the mountain. As they started the descent, relief came when the rough rocky surface became damp grass that tickled their feet. Cattle grazed and wandered sleepily on the hillside. In the distance, they could see a faint light of a farmhouse. It took a lot longer than they had first thought to reach the house, but as they got closer, they could make out three buildings. One was the farmhouse, and the others looked like barns. A dog barked as they drew close. Jason stopped to take in his surroundings.

"What's wrong?" Jean asked and put her hand on his shoulder.

"Ouch," Jason yelped, pulling away quick. "I'm burned."

"Sorry."

"I don't really know what the best thing to do is. If we call the police, how do we know Boudica's people won't find us? The local police can't really be trusted. How do we know they're not already here? I think we should hide in the barn for the night and see what's around in the daylight," Jason suggested, still trying to make out the shapes of the farmyard in the darkness.

"No, I'm thirsty and tired and want a bed. Look, he has a truck. He can drive us to a hotel," Joanne whined.

"Duh…and pay with what?" Martin interrupted.

"Jason may be right. They killed the poor French lady. They would kill the farmer without hesitation," Jean said. Her voice was harsh. She was dehydrated and tired.

They followed Jason to the barn. A few chickens clucked as they entered. The fresh smell of straw greeted them. Martin climbed up a ladder to the top of the stack.

"This will make a great bed. A bit prickly but warm." He grinned as he bounced on his knees. Jason felt around and came across a sink with a water tap. It squeaked as he turned the knob. Warm water eventually spluttered into the dusty sink. He washed his hands and face and bent down and started to drink. Jean and Joanne also drank from it like they had never drank water before.

"It's the best water I have ever tasted." Joanne smiled, running it over her hands.

Jean found a blanket. It was probably dirty, but it was so dark, who could tell? They climbed the ladder and made a large bed. Jean was in the middle with Martin and Joanne on either side of her, with Jason on the end next to Joanne. They lay close together for warmth, looking at a few stars they could see through a small hole in the barn roof.

"Why did that French lady hit Martin?" Joanne asked. "What did she call him? *Peverto* or something?" Jason looked at Martin and grinned, glad to be alive.

CHAPTER 19

BOUDICA WAS HIDING OUT in Manchester. Her underground contacts across the United Kingdom feared her but would never betray her. The Triads protected each other. An enemy of one triad was an enemy of all of them. She threw a raw chicken leg to her leopard. She had not slept much the last twenty-four hours.

The phone rang next to her bed. "Yes?" she answered.

"Boudica, it's Ping Chu. I have some bad news," the caller said nervously.

"It's all bad news." She clicked her fingernails on the small table in annoyance.

"George Young's family got away, taking the girl with them. Three of our men were killed, and several others are injured. One is serious."

"How could this happen?" Boudica shrieked. "She's a stupid housewife with a teenage son. Can't you do anything right?"

"There was someone else with them—someone who speaks Chinese. He questioned our men. He knows it was you who sent them."

"Young must have hired a good bodyguard, but Kotang will sort him out," she spat.

"They said it was a boy—a boy of about twelve with blond hair. Boudica, they say he is a demon—that he moved like lightning."

Boudica stood. She threw a table lamp against the wall and screamed in anger.

"He's not a demon, you stupid man! He's just a boy and sadly still alive. Lin Cho must have missed the little brat. It seems even *I* have now underestimated Jason Steed. I will get a message to Kotang. I want his heart brought back to me for Luke. If it's still beating when I rip it out of his pretty, little body, I will pay an extra fifty thousand. Find out where they are and await Kotang and the others. We must get that girl," she screamed and then slammed the phone down.

"Don't worry, Luke. Mummy will soon get you another boy to eat. You enjoyed Andrew Cho, didn't you? Well, this one is even younger and much prettier." She laughed and licked her blood-stained fingers.

Jean stretched her legs as she awoke in the barn. She turned to her side and looked at Martin. His eyes opened, and he smiled at her. She bent forward and kissed him.

"How did you sleep?" she whispered.

"Like a log." He yawned. She turned and looked at Joanne and Jason. Joanne was spooning Jason close for warmth. Her face was buried into the back of his neck. They were both still asleep. Jean and Martin got up and climbed down the ladder. It was getting brighter outside. They looked out a small cobweb-covered window but could see no signs of life outside. A cockerel just a few feet away screeched its morning crow, which made Jean and Martin jump.

Jason and Joanne opened their eyes. She had her arm around him and felt him move as he wiped the sleep from his eyes.

"You're nice and warm. I was cold in the night," she sighed.

"So was I," Jason said as he yawned.

Jean came back up the ladder when she heard them talking and smiled at them. "You look like two tiny lovebirds. I am going to the farmhouse. There's no one around. I'll see if I can get something to eat. I speak a little Spanish. Martin will come with me," Jean said.

Jason lifted his head and looked at her. His blond hair was a sticking up in all directions and had straw in it. He thought he should go with them, but he was cold, tired, and happy where he was for now. He enjoyed having Joanne's arm around him. It was the closest thing he had had to a hug for a long while.

Let an adult do something for a change, he told himself as he put his head back down.

Sunlight broke into the barn when Martin and Jean opened the door. Then they made their way to the farmhouse. Martin raised his hand to knock, but to his surprise, it swung open. A small, thin man with a sun-cracked face looked at them.

"Hola," he said and grinned. Jean explained that she and her son were lost, and he invited her in. Once inside, she noticed a man sitting at the table and drinking a coffee. He was huge and looked like a sumo wrestler in a suit.

Jean held Martin's hand. The big man was out of place and she was instantly nervous.

"Just the two of you?" the large man questioned.

"Yes, just me and Bobby," she lied.

"Bobby? I don't think he's called Bobby. This is the first farm-house north of your villa. I knew you would come here. George—that's his name." He put his hand inside his jacket pocket and pulled out a picture with George, Jean, and Martin and then placed it on the table.

Jean pushed Martin to the door. "Run, Martin. Run!" she screamed. Kotang caught her by her hair. He pulled her back and smashed his elbow into her face. Her limp body collapsed on the wooden floor. Kotang moved to the door, pulled out his gun, and fired a single shot that caught Martin in the back. He crashed to the dusty gravel in pain.

Jason and Joanne sat up. Jason slid down the ladder and looked out the window. He saw Martin lying on the ground, trying to crawl away. His fingers plowed through the dirt as he tried to drag his body away to safety. Then he saw Kotang striding toward Martin, the gun in his hand. Jason took the gun from his shorts and ran to the door and fired on Kotang. The distance was greater than Jason had realized. He missed with four shots, and Kotang returned fire. Jason dove back behind the door. Kotang emptied his gun of bullets into the barn. Jason ran to the window and fired again. This time, he hit Kotang in the shoulder. When Kotang fell to the ground, Jason ran back to the door and fired his last shot, his shaking hand causing him to miss again. A cloud of dirt bounced off the ground next to Kotang's leg. Kotang took out a box of .22 bullets from his pocket. He took out the clip from his gun to reload.

Don't let him reload, Jason told himself as he ran as fast as he could toward Kotang. Kotang fumbled with his gun and dropped the clip, but his swift hands soon scooped it up and slammed it into the handle of the gun. As he turned the gun, it was too late. Jason had launched himself into a flying kick aimed at Kotang's hand.

The kick was perfectly aimed. It threw the gun into the air and twenty feet away. However, Kotang was fast—his left hand catching Jason's foot. Jason fell to the ground. Kotang laughed and started dragging Jason toward him. Jason tried kicking with his other leg. He frantically wriggled, squirmed, and twisted, trying to get away. Kotang's viselike grip was strong. His right hand tightly squeezed Jason's thigh. He pulled Jason close to him, lifted the boy like a toy doll, and then grabbed Jason's throat with his huge left hand.

Immediately, he started to squeeze. Jason felt Kotang cut off his oxygen supply. His face was turning blue as he fought back. He was no match for Kotang's strength. He felt himself getting light-headed, so he closed his eyes and let his body go limp. If Kotang kept squeezing, Jason would soon be dead. He wanted to panic and fight back, but he knew if he did, Kotang would kill him.

Come on. I'm dead already. Let me go.

His lungs were bursting for air. He forced himself to stay limp, counting the seconds.

How much longer?

Kotang, thinking he had squeezed the life out of the boy, finally let him go. Jason lay motionless on the ground. Kotang pushed Jason's limp body off his leg and climbed to his feet. Slowly, Jason took a gentle breath.

Joanne started to scream. She had run to Martin and found him lying and bleeding. She kneeled down beside him, screamed for help, and pled for Martin to wake up. Kotang walked toward Joanne, holding his wounded shoulder.

"Don't worry. You won't be harmed…much," he said before he grabbed her by her hair. She turned and punched Kotang on his chest, screaming at him to let her go. She kicked, punched, and clawed at him. Kotang found it amusing. Blood ran down his left hand from the bullet wound in his shoulder. He painfully lifted his hand and grasped her throat—his huge fingers wrapping themselves around her thin, delicate neck.

"Now you be quiet or I will kill you. You're lucky. You're worth more alive than dead. Boudica needs your help," he joked.

A loud bang echoed across the farmyard, and he released his grip. Kotang's eyes rolled to the top of his head. His legs gave way under him, and his heavy body collapsed onto the gravel. A large hole in the back of his head oozed out life. Jason stood over him, his shaking hand still holding Kotang's gun. Joanne screamed more when she saw the damage to Kotang's head. Jason ran back toward the farmhouse.

A Land Rover barreled around the corner from the back of the house. The farmer, his wife, and two children sped off down the small lane toward the main road in a cloud of dust. Jason ran into the house and found Jean lying on the floor. She looked unmarked. He kneeled down and felt her wrist, trying to find a pulse. She stirred and held her face in pain.

"Martin," she called out.

"He's hurt but will live. We need to get him to a hospital.

Go and get Kotang's car," he said, pointing out the window at a black Mercedes.

"Kotang?" she asked.

"Him." Jason pointed at the body. The conversation was stopped by the sound of gunfire in the distance. They all looked down the small lane that led to the main road. Two cars had stopped the farmer's Land Rover and killed the entire family.

A black Mercedes-Benz was fast approaching the farmhouse. Jason raised his gun and opened fire at the car. It stopped, and the occupants ducked down as the windows rained broken glass on them. Jason emptied the gun on the car. By luck, it hit the fuel tank, and a huge explosion at the back of the car blew out a flume of flames. A fist of gray smoke erupted into the clear morning sky. Three men jumped free. One of them was on fire, screaming in agony while rolling on the floor, trying to suffocate the flames.

The other car stayed at the end of the drive. Jason helped Jean carry Martin and pull him across the backseat of Kotang's car. He told Joanne to sit next to Martin and apply pressure to the boy's wound to stop the bleeding. He jumped into the front passenger seat and told Jean to strap herself in.

"Now look at me and listen," he told Jean. Her hands were trembling. Her nose was still bleeding, and she was sobbing.

"Look at me!" he yelled. She was surprised by his outburst and looked at him.

"Jean, you need to be strong now for Martin's sake. I need you to drive to the nearest police station," he told her while he reloaded his gun using Kotang's box of bullets. "To the right is a wooden gate leading to the main road. This car should smash through it easily. Don't stop until you get to the police station."

She nodded and gripped the wheel. "What about you?" she asked desperately.

"Once you get through the gate, drive a few hundred yards and wait for me. But if the car is still following you, just go."

"I can't just leave you," she said.

"You may not have to. I hope I can stop the car and join you." He leaned forward and kissed her cheek. "You can do it, Jean. This is for Martin."

Jean nodded and gritted her teeth while she clenched the wheel.

A large cloud of dust erupted from the wheels of the car as she drove across the small field and broke through the gates, sending shards of wood up in the air. The two-thousand-pound car made matchsticks of the old wooden gate. As it pulled onto the main road, Jason jumped out, rolled, and ducked behind an olive tree. Jean did as she was told and drove off and stopped out of sight farther up the road.

The Triad's car wheels squealed, spitting gravel and dust as it returned to the main road in pursuit. Jason looked through the dense foliage of the small tree and took aim at the driver.

As soon as he could get a good shot, he let off three rounds. At least one hit and killed the driver. Jason ducked down, but to his horror, the car careered directly toward him. It crashed into the olive tree in front of him and knocked him down before it finally came to a stop on top of him and the tree. He was lying flat on his back under the car. It was a miracle we was not run over by the wheels. His gun was stuck fast under a tire.

He took a deep breath and wriggled his toes and fingers. To his relief, they all worked. His chest was hurting from the blow. It could have been worse. The tree seemed to have taken the brunt of it. A door opened, and he saw a pair of feet climb out of the passenger seat. The person spoke in Chinese to the others but got no response. They were either dead or unconscious.

It took Jason a few moments to come to his senses. He knew his chest was injured, although he was unsure just how bad. But he felt dampness on his leg.

I hope that's not blood and I've just peed myself, he said to himself as he felt the dampness getting worse. As he tried to slowly move, it became obvious.

It's gas.

As fast as he could, he crawled from under the car. The stunned Triad member stepped back as he watched Jason scramble out. He pointed his gun at Jason and gestured for the boy to stand. Jason pretended he was injured and pulled himself up by the rear wheel. He dug his fingernails behind the chrome hubcap and pulled it off. In one movement, he spun around and launched the hubcap like a Frisbee, aimed at the man. It flew and smacked the Triad member in the mouth. The man was momentarily stunned.

Jason pounced in that time and delivered a deadly blow to the man's windpipe. The car started to burn. The gas around him caught fire. Within seconds, the entire car was engulfed in flames. Jason had had a lucky escape. The stench of burning flesh hit Jason's senses. The others in the car were cremated. The smell reminded Jason of what Boudica had done to Kinver.

Jason ran up the road toward Jean's waiting car, holding his chest. She and Joanne had covered Martin's wound with clothing. He was now conscious and groaning in pain. They didn't say anything to Jason as he climbed in the car. They pretty much took for granted that he would take care of the Triad's thugs.

Sitting in the front seat of the car, wearing nothing but swimming shorts, Jason began shaking uncontrollably. His young body was cut, bruised, and burned from the sun—and it was taking its toll on him. He was exhausted.

As Jean started to drive off, Jason thought about his father. His eyes stung as tears ran down his cheeks. He turned his head away and looked out the window, trying to conceal his tears. For their sake, he acted tough, but inside, he was in pain and wanted nothing more than to burst out in sobs.

She drove to Malaga Hospital, where Martin was taken into the emergency ward. Jason called Interpol and then was given some basic medical treatment for his cuts. His neck and chest were badly bruised, but nothing was broken when he was given an X-ray.

Jean sat in the waiting room with Joanne. They looked up at Jason as he entered.

"I called Interpol. George had given me the number just in case," he said. "The local police will be here any second and will take me and Jo to a safe house. Jo, your father has already sent an agent from China. He will take care of you."

"What about you, Jason?" she asked.

"I will probably stay at the safe house until you are safe and they catch Boudica."

They didn't have time to say good-bye to Jean and Martin. A police car arrived, and two Spanish police officers came to collect Jason and Joanne and move them to safety.

Jason remained silent for the journey to the safe house. He didn't speak to Joanne, even when she asked if his feet felt better in his new socks and shoes. He ignored the remark and wished he was someplace else. He gently touched his neck. It was swollen and badly bruised from Kotang's attempt to kill him.

"Jason, I asked you a question. What's wrong with you? You've been like this since we left the farm," she asked.

"You mean, since you and Jean left me to fend off a car full of armed Triads that resulted in getting run over and nearly burned to death," he snapped back.

"You told her to drive off and wait."

He knew she was right, but he did not want to talk about it. He shook his head and looked away. The number of dead bodies and the constant pressure were getting to him. Even though he had washed up at the hospital, he could still smell the burning flesh of the Triads who never made it out of the car.

A message came over the radio in Spanish. The two officers looked at each other and shook their heads. One grabbed the car's radio, replied, and then turned the car around. Jason did not translate much of the conversation—something about taking them somewhere to be picked up.

As the last few houses past them and they once again came

into open countryside, Jason finally started to question what was happening.

"We should be going to a police station," he said in Spanish.

"*Sí*, but now we have orders to take you to the main highway and wait. Spanish Special Forces will take care of you."

It made sense to Jason. The local police may not have been able to protect Joanne, but he had a bad feeling in his gut. He sat back heavily in his seat and tried to relax, but something was still bothering him. An uneasy feeling snaked around his insides and gave him a tight knot in his stomach.

"Sorry," he said quietly to Joanne without looking at her.

She looked at him sympathetically and smiled. "What for? You're right, Jason. We expect too much of you."

"It's not your fault. None of this is. You can't help having an important father." He smiled back and gestured his hand to shake in friendship. Joanne took his hand and held it with both of her hands. He gave her a tight-lipped smile.

They stopped at a large service station on the main highway. A few cars were filling up with gas. Some drivers were eating inside at the café. The police car waited at the end of the parking lot.

Jason noticed a black Mercedes parked to his left. Maybe he was being paranoid. Not every driver of a black Mercedes wanted to kill him. But when a second black Mercedes stopped just a few parking places away to his right, he started to get nervous.

He noticed several Asian men dressed in the same black clothing as the hit men getting out of the car at the same time.

CHAPTER 20

"M OVE! THEY'RE TRIADS. IT'S a trap," Jason shouted.

The windscreen shattered as two bullets broke through and planted themselves in the head of the driver. The other police officer took out his gun and fired back. Joanne screamed, her hands over her head. Jason took the gun from the dead driver's holster and shot back at them. The two Triads to his left both fell. With the police officer shooting at the gunmen on the other side, Jason kicked opened his door and pulled Joanne with him, keeping low to the ground.

Another black Mercedes screeched to a halt. The doors opened, and three men with automatic weapons got out. Jason ran with Joanne down a small embankment that dropped down to a field with a few grazing cows. As he helped her over the wire fence, the sound of automatic gunfire and shattering glass came from above. The police car was riddled with 9mm bullets. The policeman was hit, his body slumped over his dead colleague.

"Run and don't stop," Jason shouted at Joanne. She did as she was told and ran off across the field.

Jason ducked down with nothing other than a small fence post to protect him. He looked at the gun he was holding—an Italian-made Beretta 92S. He took out the clip and counted five bullets.

Five bullets against all those automatic guns. I'm a goner.

He picked himself up and ran after Joanne. They may not

shoot at him if she were with him. To stay and try to fight would be foolish.

A few shots pounded the ground around him, giving him a burst of speed. He didn't stop to return fire. He figured the farther away he could get and the closer to Joanne, the safer he would be.

One of the Mercedes attempted to drive down the embankment; however, the bank proved too steep and the car slid down and became wedged under the wire fence. One got out and ran after Jason on foot. Joanne stopped and looked back. She was relieved when she saw that Jason was coming after her, but she screamed when she saw that they were being chased by one of the men.

"Jason, behind you!"

Jason glanced back and cursed. He dove to the ground and aimed his gun at the man who was getting closer.

The man wrongly assumed the boy he was chasing stumbled and fell. By the time the man saw the glint of light shining off the revolver Jason was holding, it was too late—too late to stop and too late to pull his own gun. He felt the thud against his chest before he heard the first shot. He was dead before the second shot. It sickened Jason to have to kill again.

Why do they keep coming?

He picked himself up and caught up with Joanne. In tears, she flung her arms around him when he finally reached her. For a few moments, he closed his eyes and enjoyed the luxury of a friendly hug. He looked back to see if they were being followed. The area was clear. He held her hand and continued running through the field farther away from the road and into the countryside.

The field ended with a taller wire fence that was almost six feet tall with heavy-duty wire. Without stopping to think, they climbed over it and dropped down the other side. The grass was greener, and it gave off a lush, fresh smell as they walked across the field, hand in hand.

Once again, the sun was burning into Jason's neck. He wished now he had chosen a shirt with a collar when he had been given clothing at the hospital.

"Jason, we're being watched," Joanne said and grinned.

Jason's head spun around in all directions. "Where? Who?" he gasped.

"Not who, silly. Look…a cow. She's chewing her cud and watching us."

"Chewing her what?" he asked.

"It's cud. They eat grass and then regurgitate it and chew it all over again. They have three stomachs."

"Eeew, that's gross. Remind me never to eat beef again," he said and laughed, screwing up his face.

"You drink loads of milk." She laughed back and mimicked the face he was pulling.

They carried on walking through the field. Jason kept checking to see if the Triads were still following and glanced at the cow watching them. Jason stopped in his tracks.

"That's not a cow. It's a bull," he said.

"Are you sure? Even cows can have horns."

"I may not be as smart as you, but I can tell the difference between male and female. *That* is a bull. Keep walking but faster."

"Don't be silly. It won't hurt us."

"Now we know why there's a huge wire fence. It's coming. Come on." He started jogging. Joanne was tugged along.

"Jason, it won't hurt us. Although," she said and then paused, "come to think of it, we are in Spain. You don't think they're training it for bullfighting, do you? *It's coming!*" she screamed.

The bull lowered its head and charged.

CHAPTER 21

THE GROUND SHOOK BENEATH the bull's feet as his hooves pounded the ground. Its huge, sweat-flecked body came closer and closer.

Jason pulled Joanne along. They were too far away from the fence to get out of harm's way. The bull was gaining ground and fast. The thud, thud, thud from his hooves became louder. Jason stopped, pulled the gun from his shorts, and shot at it three times. The bull's front legs gave way. Its massive head ploughed into the ground, and it came to an abrupt halt just a few feet away, steam slowly rising from its body.

"What did you do that for? The poor thing," Joanne whined.

"Are you for *real*?" he asked in disbelief. "It was gonna crush us."

"It's not the bull's fault. They train it to do that and stick him in a ring with thousands of people watching. Then they stick spears in it and tease it to make it chase people."

"You don't need to tease it. It knew what to do. Come on. We'd better keep moving," he said, throwing the empty gun away.

Girls are crazy. "*What did you do that for?*" he mimicked to himself, shaking his head.

After two hours of walking north through the Spanish countryside, they stopped and took shelter from the sun under a tree. He watched her as she closed her eyes and relaxed. The sun filtered through the branches and leaves. Her lightly tanned Asian face glistened with a thin layer of sweat. Her black hair fell delicately down her back as she tilted her head back to rest against the trunk. Her stomach started to rumble loudly.

"Oops, excuse me," she said in Chinese with half a smile. Jason smiled back at her and looked into her brown eyes. Joanne smiled and looked deep into Jason's sapphire blue eyes. His perfect white teeth stood out in the shade. His face was tanned. His blond hair was stuck up in all directions. She put her hand through his blond hair and laughed. "You need to comb this. Look, you have still got a piece of straw in it." She grinned and spoke in Chinese. Her hand plucked the straw out. Then she gently held his shoulder.

"Thanks." He paused and looked at her. For a few brief moments, the world stopped revolving and the birds stopped singing. It almost felt as if the clouds stopped drifting overhead. They said nothing. Their gaze was intense—their faces just a few inches apart. It felt so natural, but it felt forbidden too. She was a school friend of Catherine's. He was Catherine's boyfriend and a Westerner. Her father would never approve of someone like him. She broke the gaze, removed her hand, and tried to break the silence. "Your Chinese is good, although you speak it with an English accent," she joked.

"Your English is good, although you speak it with a Chinese accent," he said and grinned.

"Why couldn't we stay with Jean and Martin or now go direct to a police station?"

"We can't trust them. They knew we were at the villa, so they must have inside information. Someone working for SYUI has betrayed us. We now know they have connections here, as they gave the orders to those poor policemen," he said and sighed. "Come on. We'd better get moving. I want to get far away from here." He forced himself up onto his tired legs—his muscles complaining as he did. He pulled Joanne up. As they walked, she held his hand. He looked at her and she was crying again.

"What did I say?"

She stopped and burst out in tears and hugged Jason. "Martin…he might die because of me," she cried.

Jason held her tightly, trying to think of something to say but nothing he could think of would be appropriate. "No, I think he will be okay, but if he dies, it's because of Boudica."

Back in London, Raymond Steed arrived at SYUI with Scott in tow to find out where exactly they had taken his son. Ray was surprised how many police and SYUI officers knew Scott on a first-name basis.

"How much time have you spent here?" Ray asked as they climbed a flight of stairs.

"I was here every day when Jase was in juvie. I wanted to know everything that was happening. I want a job here when I grow up. This place is amazing."

"How did Jason cope with juvie?"

"He hated it. He had to fight his way through it. Every time I saw him, his knuckles were cut and split. But that wasn't the worst part. Every time I visited him and it was time for me to leave, he got upset. You could see it in his eyes. They welled up. He hated staying there."

Inside the SYUI department, they bumped into George, who was coming out of the men's room and wiping his hands on his pants. He immediately noticed Scott and smiled.

"All right, mate. How's it going?" he asked. Then he stuttered when he noticed Raymond Steed. "Mr. Steed, I, um…did not know you were back. Nice to see ya again." George gulped, holding his hand out for Ray.

"Where is Jason?" Ray said, coming straight to the point.

"Let's have a chat. Fancy a brew?" George asked, gesturing to the coffeepot.

"No thanks." They followed George into his office. He tipped some files off a chair facing his desk so Ray could sit. Slowly, he walked around to his desk and sat looking at Ray.

"Jason's with my wife and son in my villa in Spain. We also have the daughter of the Chinese commissioner there. I did it for their safety. Yeah, and I know before you say it. It's my fault he had to leave the country, I know. My own family is at risk. The Triads want revenge for bringing Boudica's empire down. It's cost them millions. We have temporarily lost contact with me misses. They've probably gone fishing or shopping," he said, slightly concerned.

"When did you last talk to them?" Scott asked.

"Two days ago, but you know what women are like—"

"They were supposed to call every day," Scott snapped back. Ray looked shocked, looked back at George, raised his eyebrows, and asked for an explanation.

"All right, keep your hat on. We called the local police, who said they would drop in and say hello. They should be reporting back any second. I'll get that brew I promised and see if they've heard anything. Scott, show Mr. Steed around," George said, climbing out from behind his desk.

When George came back, he was as white as a sheet and sat heavily into a chair, looking straight ahead but not focusing on anything.

"You had better start telling me what's going on, George," Ray shouted.

George got up, loosened his tie, and ran his hand through his greasy hair. He looked at Ray. "They found three dead bodies at my villa—Boudica's men. They also found the neighbor, a French woman, shot dead. My wife and the kids are gone. They are still looking at the scene, but there may be some good news. Two of the dead men had been shot, but the third had no marks on him. They are going to examine his body," George said. He was now sweating more than usual.

"Why is that good news?" Ray snapped back.

"I can only think of one person who can kill with his bare hands. We both know who that is," George said, forcing a smile.

"Jason Steed strikes again," Scott said and punched the air in triumph so hard he could have left a bruise. The adults around him looked down at him. His remark was in bad taste, but that was typical Scott.

"When will we know more?" Ray asked.

"The Spanish Police are searching the whole area now. They will find them. Mrs. Young has probably just moved to a safer place. It's now a full-scale murder investigation," he said.

By late afternoon, Jason and Joanne stumbled across a railway track and followed it north. Whenever they heard a train approaching, they would hide behind shrubs and vegetation so they could keep out of sight. They had no idea who they were hiding from, but they felt safer being out of sight. The sun was hotter today, and the jagged terrain all seemed the same.

They eventually came upon a tiny railroad station. Tired, they decided it would be safe enough to board.

"If this is correct, the train will be here in half an hour. I'll get two tickets," Jason said, digging in his pocket for the money Interpol had given him for snacks. His voice was slightly hoarse, and he rubbed his throat, which was severely bruised from the stranglehold Kotang had had him in yesterday.

Jason smiled as he helped Joanne up into the carriage. He looked over her shoulder and noticed a figure duck behind a wall. Jason looked up and down the platform but could not see the man again. Joanne left Jason looking out the window and went to find a seat. Slowly, the train started to pull out. Jason noticed that four men ran for the train. They opened the door much to the objection of the guard and jumped on.

CHAPTER 22

Unaware, Joanne had already gone off down the corridor. Jason wanted to jump off, but she was gone. His face turned white as he ran down the corridor with a sense of dread and looked through the windows of the compartments. He got to the end of the carriage and went into the first-class section. He continued running down the corridor and looking through the windows. Then he saw her taking a seat in a sleeping compartment.

"Where did you go? Are you stupid or what? We have to get off. Come on," he shouted as he grabbed her arm. He took her to the main doors and opened them. They had already left the platform and started moving a lot faster.

"I can't jump down there," Joanne protested.

"Stay here," he said. He opened the door, and before she could protest, he was gone. Rather than wait for the Triads to attack, he would go after them. He looked down the corridor, and he saw that it was still clear. He could not yet see them. They were still a few carriages back, working their way forward. Jason opened the sleeping compartments and searched for anything he could use as a weapon. In the first compartment, he found a lady sleeping. He looked at her belongings but could not see anything he could use, so he moved onto the next. A young couple lay on the bed, smoking.

"Get out. This is private," they shouted in Spanish.

"Sorry," Jason said and smirked. The next sleeping compartment he checked was empty. As he made his way to the end of the carriage, he could now see ahead. The four men dressed in black would soon be in his carriage. They slammed every door as they rapidly worked their way forward. Jason quickly ran back to the sleeping compartment with the lady. He opened the door and went through her belongings. He picked up a can of hair spray. He then ran to the next compartment with the young couple. Again, they protested and tried to cover up. Jason quickly ran and made a grab for the cigarette lighter. Then he ran back out.

Jason ducked into the empty compartment. He closed the door, pulled down the fold-up bed, jumped on it, and closed it with him hiding inside. The train slowed down a little when the track took a steep turn around a mountain. Above his racing heartbeat, he heard the door opening and voices. They were in the compartment with him. Not leaving anything to chance, they lowered the folding bed and were taken by surprise. Jason sprayed the hair spray at them and lit the cigarette lighter. A huge ball of flame burst out in their direction. Two men screamed out in pain. One ran out of the compartment, holding his face. The other fell back against the window. Jason jumped down and threw a roundhouse kick at the man, knocking the wind out of him. He dropped his gun and fell to his knees and held his eyes in pain. Jason grabbed the gun and turned. The other man was moaning and holding his eyes in pain.

The air was filled with the ghastly smell of burnt hair and singed flesh. Jason crawled on his elbows to the doorway, the gun in front of him. As he got to the door, he could see the leg of another man creeping slowly toward the door. The train entered a tunnel. The dim lights gave Jason the chance to see the man's reflection in the window. He was getting closer—a gun aimed at the doorway. The two blinded men continued moaning and asking for help. Jason lurched forward, took aim, and fired a single shot at the man. The bullet hit his chest, and the impact from the German P32 gun threw the man back down the corridor, where he now lay motionless. Jason jumped to his feet and looked for the fourth man, who was nowhere to be seen.

He grabbed one of the blinded men by the arm.

"I'll help you. We need to wash your eyes. Come with me to the bathroom," Jason spat. He guided the man down the corridor and opened the main door to the carriage. Without a second thought, Jason shoved him off train. He went back and did the same to the second blinded man. Once both injured men were off the train, he decided to throw the dead Triad's body off the train too. He hated touching the dead man's hands, but he pulled the body back down the corridor. He was heavy, but slowly, Jason made progress. Once he got the body to the doorway, he started to push it out of the train.

He sensed something behind him. He turned and saw the fourth man kicking out at him. Jason blocked the kick, but the momentum pushed him back and almost out of the door. He held on with one hand, trying to crawl back over the body that was now almost fully out the door. The man kicked again at Jason and caught him in the face, knocking the boy back farther. Jason scrambled to stay on the train. The body that Jason was kneeling on fell out and rolled down the bank.

Jason pulled himself back in, but the man was kicking and punching him still. As more punches caught Jason's face, he made the extreme decision to jump and take the man with him. He couldn't risk leaving the man on the train to find Joanne. Jason grabbed the man's wrist, and with a judo technique, he pulled the man out of the train with him. Immediately, Jason let go and rolled up into a ball, covering his head with his arms and spinning through the air. For the smallest of moments, as he gained the highest point of his leap, Jason seemed to hover above the tracks, as if gravity itself had paused.

Crunch! He landed on his back in gravel. He skidded along the ground and grazed the skin off his unprotected legs and back. Once he came to a stop, he sprang to his feet and got his bearings. He ran at the moving train as fast as he could. He didn't stop to see what had happened to the man he had pulled off. His heart pounded against his chest as he forced himself to sprint faster than he ever had before.

The last carriage was the mail carriage. Jason ran toward it but found nothing he could grab hold of. Then he saw it. Right at the very end of the approaching carriage, a metal handle stuck out. Jason dived. It smacked against the palms of his hand hard, and in lightning speed, he clasped his hands tightly around the handle. He was picked up and flapping like a kite in the wind. As he dangled, he was unsure how long he could hold on for. The wind pushed his body back and made him feel heavier. He could just see the very back of the carriage. There was a metal service ladder that led to the top of the carriage.

It was too far around to grab with his other hand. He was

stuck. He yelled out in anger and frustration. He turned his back to the train and curled his legs back. The train had now started to speed up again, and the wind was fighting him.

As he felt the pain and knew he had reached the last reserves of his strength, Jason managed to hook his feet around the ladder. It took the weight off his hands, but he now had to let go with his hands and try to hold on to the ladder with just his feet. He was bent around the back corner of the carriage. He didn't stop to think. He was getting tired and had to act fast. If his feet slipped, he would fall and Joanne would be gone. And at the speed the train was moving now, he could get killed. He let go and pulled himself around the edge of the carriage by using his stomach muscles. His muscles screamed in pain, but he just managed to catch the ladder with his hands. Once he had his body supported by the ladder, he could finally rest a bit.

The mail carriage had no back doors. The only way Jason could rejoin the passenger carriages was to go up and over the roof. He climbed the ladder and made it to the top of the train. The wind was stronger than he had imagined. He had to keep low.

It's not like this in the films, he said to himself as tiny pieces of dust and grit went into his eyes and blinded him.

Tears poured from his eyes. He tried wiping them, but the tears and his dirty, grease-covered hands just made them worse—his face even dirtier. Jason crawled on all fours along the roof of the mail carriage. He had to close his eyes to prevent more dust stinging them. The railcar seemed to go on forever. Eventually, he made it to the end and was pleased to find another metal ladder at the end. He climbed down between the mail carriage and the passenger carriage. He jumped across. The last passenger carriage was the dining car.

Jason opened the door and entered. It was full of people seated at tables with white tablecloths, drinking and eating. There was a hum of chatter and soft classical music in the background. As Jason started to walk through the car, the hum of chatter got quieter and quieter until there was silence. Jason noticed that everyone stopped what they were doing and stared at him. Why, he did not know.

"Where did you come from?" a waiter asked in Spanish, looking down his nose at Jason.

"Do you have a ticket?" a train guard asked as he walked toward Jason. Everyone in the carriage was now staring at Jason. He felt the pocket of his shorts, and to his relief, he found the two tickets he had bought. He passed one to the guard. As he did, he noticed his hands and forearms. They were black with dirt and grease from the ladder. He looked down and noticed that he had blood and dirt on his shirt. His legs were dirty and cut. His shorts were ripped open down one side. He could only imagine what his face was like.

"You are traveling alone?" the guard asked.

"No, of course not. You don't think my parents would let me go on a long trip on a train alone, do you?"

"Why do you look like that? What happened?"

"I fell over."

"You can't be on the train like that."

"I didn't see a dress code when I bought the ticket," Jason protested, snatching his ticket back from the startled guard. "Sorry, but I was told not to talk to strangers."

He walked out of the dining car, and everyone's eyes followed him. Once he was in the next carriage, he started to run from carriage to carriage until he came to the first-class carriage. The exit door was still open. Jason closed it and noticed a trail of blood where he had dragged the dead body. He went to the compartment to check on Joanne. His heart sank. It was empty.

CHAPTER 23

J OANNE!"

"Jason, in here," came a muffled shout. She was hiding in the fold-up bed. He opened it. She had been crying again. Her eyes were red and puffy. She climbed down and hugged him so tightly he could not breathe.

"Don't you ever leave me again! I heard a gunshot. I thought you were dead," she said and sobbed. After recent events, he welcomed the closeness of a hug. He held his cheek close to her neck and closed his eyes. Together, they felt safe. He noticed she was trembling, and it seemed to be getting worse.

"What's wrong?" he asked. She didn't reply. She just continued to shake. He stepped back to look at her. She looked away. Was she…smirking?

"What?" he asked, bewildered and annoyed. With that, she burst out laughing, shaking her head at the same time, trying to apologize.

"Sorry," she said, trying to stop herself from laughing.

"What is it?" he asked again, perplexed.

"You," she said and laughed. "Just look at yourself." She took his hand and marched outside to find a restroom. She squeezed in and pulled Jason with her. Reluctantly he followed. He looked at the image in the mirror. He saw a boy with a black face. One ear was filthy. His body was covered in brown dirt, oil, blood, and grease, and his shorts were ripped at the side all the way to the elastic waist, revealing part of his buttock. His legs were dirty, scratched, and cut. One of his eyes was black where he had tried to wipe the grit out with dirty hands. Jason smiled at first and then he seemed annoyed; however, he soon burst out laughing too. They laughed and tried as much as they could to clean him up in the small sink.

Joanne helped wash Jason's ear. The restroom on the train was not really big enough for two people. Joanne laughed at him as he complained that she was scrubbing his ear too hard with a tiny green bar of soap. She managed to wash most of the grease off him, but his torn clothing was ruined. They continued the journey in the safety of the sleeper compartment. The train stopped at Madrid briefly and set off again, eventually stopping at Zaragoza in northern Spain.

As they stepped off the train, Jason noticed several local police standing at the end of each platform. Two police officers close to Jason spoke on a radio and looked at the two young children. Jason's filthy shirt and ripped shorts stood out. He took Joanne's hand and briskly walked up the platform. The taller policeman let out a deep sigh, his lips fluttering, and started to walk cautiously toward Jason.

"Excuse me. May I have a word?" the police officer asked in Spanish.

Jason turned and smiled at the man. "Hola," he said.

"Can you children give me your names?"

"I am Pepe. This is my girlfriend, Wen. We can't stop. We have to meet our parents outside the station," Jason said in his best Spanish, still walking and tugging on Joanne's hand. The police officer signaled two other officers over.

"Maybe we can escort you outside," he said, getting closer.

Jason kept moving and tried to ignore him.

"Wen, you seem a little worried. Is everything all right?" he asked Joanne.

"She does not speak Spanish. We are not supposed to talk to strangers," Jason replied.

The officer was now next to Jason and bearing down on them. "Please stop. I need to talk to you," he said, placing a hand on Joanne's shoulder. Jason gripped Joanne's hand tighter. "Come with us. We have been looking for you. It seems you have left a trail of dead bodies behind you. My superiors wish to question you."

Jason stopped and looked around. On the next platform, a busy local commuter train was unloading. The platform was full of people rushing in all directions, including a large group of schoolchildren in uniform complete with hats.

"Do you trust me, Jo?" Jason asked in Chinese so the police could not understand.

She looked at him and nodded.

Jason spun around on his right foot and kicked out with his left, knocking the police officer over. He ran, pulling Joanne with him, and then jumped down onto the tracks. They ran across the tracks and climbed up the other side onto the busy platform. The policemen started shouting and blowing their whistles. He kept running into the crowd. They sprinted down the platform hand in hand, dodging the other passengers, their small size hidden by the adults. They soon reached the end of the platform. This led out onto the main train station. It was rush hour and packed with commuters. Without giving any warning, Jason pulled Joanne into the men's bathroom.

"You nearly pulled my arm out of its socket," Joanne panted.

"*Oi!*" a schoolboy protested at the sight of Joanne in the men's toilets. Jason grabbed the boy by the face and pushed him back into a cubicle and then squeezed the boy's cheeks with his thumb and fingers.

"Jo, come in and shut the door," Jason ordered. The boy was terrified. He was a little bigger than Jason but could see the look in Jason's eyes.

"Okay, we can do this easy or hard. I'm taking your clothes. Get undressed." The boy shook his head. Jason grabbed his nose and twisted it. "I will not ask again. Get undressed." The boy slowly undid his tie. Jason helped undress the boy.

"Not my pants," the boy protested. "She is in here." Again, Jason pulled the boy's nose.

"I don't want to hurt you, but if I have to, I will. Take everything off. You can keep your underwear." The boy passed his clothes to his attacker. He also took his shoes and socks. "The shoes fit. We're going outside now. You stay here for five minutes. If you come out any sooner, I'll thump you. Here, put these on." He passed the boy his own torn shorts. Jason took Joanne by the hand once more and went back outside onto the platform.

"Look, a girl your size. We need her clothes. Come on," he said, pulling Joanne through the crowd. He smashed the glass on the fire alarm and pressed it. The alarms sounded like air raid sirens. People started screaming and running in all directions. It was chaos. When he got close to the girl, he put his arm around her.

"Quick! There's a fire, but I know a way out." Jason said in Spanish. The shocked girl had no time to protest. She was whisked away and taken into the ladies' bathroom. Jason marched the stunned girl into a cubicle with Joanne and said, "She needs your uniform. Take it off."

"No, let me go," she protested.

Jason looked at Joanne. "Do something," he said, holding the girl.

"I can't hit her," Joanne argued.

"Neither can I. I can't hit a girl." The Spanish schoolgirl started to fight back and dug her fingernails into Jason's arm. He grabbed the side of her neck with his right hand, dug his fingers into her main artery, which carried the blood to the brain, and squeezed. She fought back and bit his forearm, but soon, she fainted. He caught her and sat her on the toilet. "Get her clothes on."

"If you promise not to watch." She soon undressed the girl and slipped the uniform on herself.

They emerged from the bathroom in school uniform. They mixed into the crowd of passengers and a large group of noisy schoolchildren all trying to exit the station in panic. Nobody gave them a second glance.

Jason looked at the train they should have caught to Santander, but it was crowded with police. He noticed a train that was headed to Bordeaux in France and chose that. Using money he found in the schoolboy's pocket, he bought two tickets and boarded the train.

"You look smart in uniform. Do you have to wear a uniform at the school you go to?" Joanne asked.

"Yeah."

"How many different languages do you speak?"

"Chinese, Japanese, Spanish, French, and I'm learning German. Have you any idea where we're heading?"

"Not a clue. Everything was in Spanish."

"We're going to France. Probably have a problem at the border. No passports."

"Why did you run from the police? Surely they can contact my dad or your SYUI unit."

"I don't trust anyone. I trust SYUI but no one else. The Triads seem to know where we are all the time. They are everywhere. The only way to stay alive is to keep moving." Jason sat back in the seat. His stomach was screaming for food and he was tired.

"I feel bad about what I did to that boy. I hate bullies and that's what I just did."

"But he was bigger than you."

"I know. His pants are too big and keep falling down." Jason laughed and pulled out some chewing gum from a pocket. "That was nice of him. He left us some gum. Want some, Wen?"

A few hours later, the chief commander of SYUI got a call from the prime minister, who had spoken to the Spanish secretary of state. It was not a pleasant call.

Commander Caldwell was informed that Jason and Joanne

had been sighted at Zaragoza train station but had again managed to escape. Caldwell was a tall, gray-haired man in his late fifties. He had never personally taken a liking to George and his manner, but he had been impressed with the job Young was doing at SYUI—until now.

Caldwell marched into SYUI and headed straight for Young's office. "I will be brief, George. First, I am very sorry to hear about your son. I do hope he makes a full recovery. However, we now have an international mess that is of your creation! The *prime minister* has just told me in no uncertain terms to finish this now and stop Steed's path of bloody destruction!"

"What? The bloody Triads are doing the bleeding killing," George protested.

"Hardly, George. The Spanish police have just found more bodies alongside a rail track. Plus, at Zaragoza main train station, *your* inside man assaulted a police officer and two children!

"The prime minister is outraged that we are behind it. What can you tell me about the Spanish farmer and his family? Did Jason kill them too? The local people want answers—and to be quite frank, so do I."

"Jason did *not* kill the farmer and his family. We found the body of Kotang, a Triad-hired killer. Plus, the bodies of more Triads just outside the farm. My wife says they were being followed. It's a miracle that Jason has managed to keep Joanne safe. He saved my family's life!"

"Then why did he attack the Spanish police officer?"

"He doesn't trust anyone, let alone the local police. Let's face it—last time they had him and Joanne 'safe,' they were attacked.

I thought for sure he had been captured, but it seems even I have underestimated the boy."

"We need to rein him in before any more people are killed. Can you make contact?"

"No, he has our code number and will call when it's safe to do so."

Caldwell shook his head in disgust. "George, sorry, but I'm taking you off the operation. It's got out of hand and now my job is on the line. I'm going to send Steed's picture and passport information to all the Spanish border stations and pray for both our sakes he's apprehended. I want you to go to a safe house. You're in no condition to run things here—and *that's* an order."

CHAPTER 24

I T WAS LATE AFTERNOON when the train stopped at the French and Spanish border where all passengers had to disembark and walk through customs. Jason and Joanne searched for a telephone.

"I don't have any money to call," Jason said glumly when he noticed a pay phone to Joanne. She pulled her hand out of her jacket pocket and handed Jason a handful of coins.

"Look what I found. Don't use them all. I need a drink."

"Then we should have taken the uniform from a richer girl." Jason laughed as he marched toward the phone. He dialed the international code and SYUI office.

"I need to speak to George Young. This is Jason Steed."

After a long pause, a voice answered. "Jason?"

"George…I'm sorry. I did everything I could. The Triads are everywhere. Kotang had a gun. I was with Joanne when they shot Martin." He was interrupted.

"Jason, I know you did everything you could, son. Is Joanne okay?"

"I won't let anything happen to her. I promise. They will have to kill me first. I will bring her home safe. George, I'm sorry. I really tried to protect Martin. Is he okay?" Jason voice started to break. He was tired and was still feeling guilty. He fought with his emotions.

"It's okay, Jason. Martin is off the critical list now. He is expected to make a full recovery. I want you to hand yourself in to the local police. We have to trust them."

There was a long silence.

"It's over?"

"No, Boudica got away. We think she's in France, but we can't go hunting for her in another country. If I had my way, we would storm straight up to Mont Blanc and fish her out of her lair. The Triads are gathering in there to plan their next move now that we've shut down the Coco-Bites factory.

"I'm sorry I got you into this, Jason. The Spanish police can keep you safe. Just don't talk to anyone else. Whatever you do, keep the girl safe. If not, this will all have been for nothing. But hand yourself in. Don't run from the Spanish police anymore."

"If you say so," he said and sighed.

"I do say so. Your father will be pleased you are safe."

"He's away at sea."

"No, Jason, he came home. He gave me a hard time for using you."

"Damn it. I'm going to be in so much trouble!" With that remark, George started to laugh. "What's so funny?"

"Jason, you've killed a dozen Triads and assaulted a police officer and two kids. You have half the bleeding villains around the world trying to kill you. Plus, you are on the Spanish police's 'Most Wanted' list, and all you are worried about is being in trouble with your dad!"

"I guess when you say it like that, it does sound trivial." The phone started beeping. "We have no more money. I'll do as you say." The phone cut off.

Joanne was sitting on the floor cross-legged with her arms folded. Her eyes were almost closed. Jason bent down and took her arm, gently pulling her up.

"Come on," he said. "Let's get something to eat and drink."

"You still have some money left?"

"We won't need any. The good Spanish people will buy it for us." Jason noticed a policeman near the checkpoint. Jason introduced himself. The stunned policeman called on his radio. Within five minutes, the station was full of police sirens and flashing blue lights.

The police tried to separate them, but Joanne screamed and held Jason's hand so tightly she almost cut off his circulation. They allowed them to travel to the police station together, but once at the station, they were separated and given food and drink. Jason was led into a small interview room. It had no windows, a table, and three chairs. Jason sat on a chair and waited for nearly two hours. Eventually he fell asleep with his head on his forearms on the table. He was woken by a loud, deliberate cough.

"Hola," a man in a suit said. Jason just nodded. He looked the man up and down. He was thin with dark Mediterranean skin, slick, greasy black hair, and dark brown eyes. The broad shadow of the Spanish police detective loomed over Jason, who still had his head down and eyes half-closed.

He leaned in from behind—his breath going down the neck of the boy's shirt and his mouth close to Jason's ear. "You say you are Jason Steed, but you tell others you are called Pepe. To me, you say only the truth. You look so small for a mass murderer."

Jason could smell alcohol on his breath.

"Can we speak in English? I thought you called me a mass murderer," Jason said and laughed.

"Your Spanish is very good, Jason. That is what I called you," he said, now in broken English.

"You're joking, right? I haven't murdered anyone. I defended myself."

"Maybe that is true. Maybe it's not. But if it is, why did you run from the police and steal clothing?"

"Duh! Maybe it's because people shooting are trying to kill us. I didn't know who to trust. Besides, the last policemen who were looking after us got killed. I'm not saying any more until SYUI gets here."

"SYUI?" he said and laughed. "They aren't coming. George Young has been relieved of duty for the mess he caused. You are on your own now. I suggest you cooperate with us, and we can close this."

A knock at the door came, and a uniformed policeman entered.

"Sir, the girl. She will not speak to us. She is crying and screaming at everyone. She demands to see the boy," he said in Spanish. Jason got up from his seat.

"Let me see her," he ordered.

"Señor Steed, we need to interview you separately to make sure your stories are the same."

"Unless I see her now, I will not say another word to you. I'm a minor. My father should be here and his lawyer. Let me see her and we will tell you everything you want to know," Jason pleaded. After a brief pause, Jason was taken down the corridor. He could hear Joanne screaming his name and crying from a room farther down. He ran into the room and found her on the floor with her arms around her knees. Her face was red and covered in tears.

George left Scotland Yard offices in the back of an unmarked police car. He was being driven to a safe house in East London. He looked at his watch and wondered how long it had been since he had last eaten.

Two single gunshots rang out. The car swerved and hit the back of a double-decker bus. George was thrown to the floor.

"You okay, mate?" George asked as he lifted himself off the floor. Blood trickled down the driver's face from a black hole in his forehead. George was now certain someone on the inside was giving information to the Triads. He was in an unmarked vehicle, and only a few people at SYUI knew where he was heading.

The back door was opened, and a gun was stuck into George's round stomach. He raised his hands and slowly climbed out. Three masked gunmen gestured for him to follow. He was thrown onto the floor of a waiting van. The doors slammed shut. He felt a sharp pain in his leg from a syringe and then nothing.

Simon Caldwell called an emergency meeting with the secretary of state. He sat at the head of the table in a dimly lit room. Secretary Nigel Raw sat at the other end, and Metropolitan police commissioner John Lock sat in the center, alongside two SYUI officers.

"Young has been taken and, we suspect, killed. The good news is that Coco-Bites is off the shelves. There is no telling how many lives have been saved by the operation. In every battle, we lose a few soldiers. It's unavoidable no matter how sad," Caldwell spoke calmly and directly.

"The Steed boy and Lin Tse-Hsu's daughter, they are in custody?" Secretary Raw asked.

"Yes, the Spanish authorities have them."

"What do you have planned for them?"

"The girl can be returned to her father in China. Let them protect her. A top Chinese agent is on his way there now. However, Jason Steed is a bigger problem. He is still top on the Triad's hit list. It's not nice to say this, but it would have been easier if he had been removed by the Triads. Then this would be over."

He continued, "I will be straight to the point. We can't afford any more innocent people getting killed. It may be better for everyone concerned if he had an accident."

"But Jason Steed is a national hero. He's already the youngest person in Britain to be awarded the Victoria Cross and the Queens Award for Bravery. Not to mention he has a close connection with the royal family," Police Commissioner Lock argued. He was outraged by the suggestion.

"This won't be over until Boudica gets her revenge! Once he is out of the picture, things will quiet down again. In all battles, there are casualties," Simon Caldwell grunted.

"You have got to be joking, man," Commissioner Lock protested. "The boy is a hero. If this got out, I don't want to think what could happen. Her Majesty still has a lot of power. How could you explain this to her?"

Secretary Raw interrupted, "Unless you have anything else to suggest, leave it to Caldwell and his office to tidy up. We need Steed back in British custody ASAP—one way or another." Raw gave Caldwell a pointed look.

John Lock jumped up from his seat, knocked his chair over, and stormed out of the meeting as he shook his head.

CHAPTER 25

JASON AND JOANNE WERE asleep in a Spanish cell when a huge explosion rocked the police station. Jason woke instantly. He put on his shoes and looked outside the cell door. Smoke started billowing down the corridor. Several gunshots broke the silence. He turned to wake Joanne and almost knocked her over. She had her shoes on and was right behind him.

More gunshots split the night silence. The Triads had launched a full-scale attack on the police station. Armed with just revolvers, the Spanish police fought back against the Triads, who were heavily armed and prepared.

"It's time to go," Jason said, taking her hand. She looked up at him adoringly.

They ran up the stairs toward the fire escape. As they headed for it, the doors blew in with a terrific explosion, momentarily deafening them and covering them in dust and smoke. Jason pulled Joanne to the ground in the corner. He noticed two dark figures with guns running into the room. The dust and smoke from the explosion hid them as they crouched down. Once they passed, Jason tugged at Joanne, and they ran toward the exit through the smoke. Once in the street, gunshots and sirens could be heard from all directions. They ran from the building and up a narrow street, but as they turned a corner, a masked gunman stood in their path. Jason let go of Joanne's hand and ran at him.

Before the man could raise his gun, Jason launched into a flying kick and caught the man in the face, sending him to the ground. Jason leapt to his feet and pounced on the man. He threw a right fist at the man's throat and crushed his windpipe. He grabbed the man's gun and fled with Joanne.

As they turned the corner of another street, two more gunmen blocked their way. Jason didn't hesitate. He opened fire. The German-made Lugar pistol hit its target. Both men fell to the ground. As they passed them, Joanne picked up a gun and passed it to Jason.

A handsome, well-groomed Asian man wearing a white suit and a black, opened-necked shirt stepped out of a silver-colored Porsche. He slowly placed his Ray-Ban sunglasses in his jacket pocket and closed his car door. Jason noticed him and held his revolver ready. The man pulled out a gun from inside his jacket. Jason raised his gun to shoot and yelled in pain when the man shot Jason's gun from his hand. Jason released his grip on Joanne and ran at the man, not knowing if he had enough time to hit him before the man fired again. As Jason leapt into the air to kick, the man placed his gun back in his pocket and blocked Jason's attack. Jason counterattacked and swept the man's feet away from him, sprawling him out on the road's surface. He looked surprised to have been taken down by a boy. As Jason tried to pounce, the man rolled away and pulled out his gun, pointed it in Jason's direction, and fired twice.

This is the end, Jason told himself as he ducked. He felt no pain though. Shooting erupted from behind him as Triads fired at Jason. He turned to see one lying on the floor and two others shooting. The man in white opened fire and shot them both through the hearts. Jason glanced across at Joanne, who was kneeling down with her hands over her ears.

Another melee of automatic gunfire came from the other end of the street. The mystery man in white leapt onto the hood of his car and killed the assassin with great accuracy. He reminded Jason of his hero, Bruce Lee. Jason pulled Joanne to her feet. He had no idea who the man was, but he had to trust him. He could have killed them easily if he had wanted to.

"When I say to take her and run, go and I'll find you," he instructed Jason, who was ducking down for cover with Joanne next to a car.

A flurry of bullets hit the street again. The man kept his cool and fired accurately, picking off the attackers one by one.

"Now run and don't stop!" he shouted as he took a second gun from inside his jacket and then used both guns for covering fire.

Jason took Joanne's hand and ran down the street. The shooting soon ceased behind them. The man had finally been hit, and he was now lying on the ground—a large red patch spreading across the back of his white jacket. Again, the man in white reloaded and fired at the Triads. Jason glanced back. His eyes met the eyes of the fallen man. Jason would never be able to explain the look, but it told him to keep going and not to give up. Bullets pounded the wounded man's body. The sight angered Jason. He admired how the stranger had fought to the very end.

When Jason got to the corner, another Triad gunman ran out in front of him. Unfortunately for the gunman, he was only a few feet away from Jason. Jason released Joanne's grip and threw a makiwara punch at the man's chest. It was one of the most powerful punches in karate. He kept his momentum going, and just before impact, he twisted his hips and shoulder into his two-knuckled fist. He gave an ear blasting "keeah" as he hit the man. The impact broke the man's rib bones, sending one directly into his heart. Jason collapsed on top of his victim and then held his hand, which had been wounded during the impact. Joanne bent down, picked up the man's gun, and handed it to Jason as she helped him to his feet.

She's getting good at this, he said to himself, trying to shake the pain from his hand.

They ran down an alley hand in hand and emerged into a busy street directly in the path of an oncoming a Coca-Cola truck. It swerved to miss the two children and hit a small Renault traveling in the other direction. Cars screeched to a halt and sounded horns. A bus smashed into the back of the small Fiat car that crashed into a lamppost. A Vespa scooter swerved, rode up the pavement, and knocked into a flower stall.

A woman screamed in horror when she saw that Jason had a gun in his hand. They passed the angry crowd and several streets of homes until they came to a busier part of the city. They skirted around the streets and ducked between buildings. He didn't look back but ran faster than he had ever run in his life. Somehow, Joanne kept on her feet as he pulled her along. They continued to sprint between cars and motorcycles. Jason tucked his gun down his pants. They stopped running and walked briskly among the crowds. The two youngsters were out of breath and red-faced.

He noticed a man filling his car with gas when the man left to go inside and pay. Jason and Joanne climbed in the back and ducked down under the seats. The man climbed back in and sat heavily in his chair. Jason fought the panic and tried to breathe as shallowly as he could. His heart thudded in his ears. Joanne put her hand over her mouth but could not stop panting, which the driver heard.

"What are you doing in my car? Get out or I'll call the police," he ordered. Jason stuck the gun in the balding man's neck and spoke Spanish.

"Drive north. Just do as I say. Please don't make me kill anyone else tonight." The man looked at Jason and noticed his eyes. The boy did not look like he was joking, and the cold metal from the gun in his neck was very real. He nervously started the car and drove north.

"You take my car. I have some money. Please don't shoot me. I have children," he begged. Jason studied him and noticed the man had a red drinker's nose and watery eyes.

"Hello, do I look like I can drive? Just do as I say and you won't get hurt. If you want to see your children again, just do as I say." Jason sat back in the seat and took the gun out of the man's neck. Joanne said nothing. She gazed out the window and looked at the Spanish town as if this were all a bad dream.

After three hours, the driver slowed down and pulled to the side of the road. It was a county road with no streetlights. Nothing could be seen outside without the lights. Moths and insects danced outside in the beam of the car lights.

"Why have you stopped?" Jason questioned.

"We are about a mile from the border, and they will search the car. I have some things best not seen by customs," he spoke slowly and calmly.

"What things?"

"Things children must not see. *Even* children with guns. Adult things."

"*What* things?" Jason asked again, putting the gun in the man's neck.

"Adult books with pictures. I sell it to special clients."

"You mean porn?" Jason snorted.

"*Sí*," the man said.

"Where are we?"

"Candanchu. It's a small border town. Two miles beyond are the Pyrenees Mountains."

"Does the village have a train?"

"*Sí*, but it only goes south. It does not go through the Pyrenees. The town is small—a few hotels for skiing, a few shops and homes, and a small airport."

"How far is the airport?"

"It's not that sort of airport. It's a tiny airport with small planes—nothing commercial. We are close to the airport now. It's over to your right. You will find maybe two hangars and a few small planes. It has a small grass runway."

"What's your name, sir?" Jason asked.

"Juan Martinez."

"Well, Señor Martinez, this is where we leave you. Drive home and say nothing to anyone. If you do, I will let it be known that Juan Martinez sells illegal porn."

They climbed out of the car and watched Juan turn his car around. The sound of his car slowly faded. The red taillights grew smaller until they too faded, leaving them in total darkness. Slowly, as their eyes became used to the darkness, they walked toward the airport. A soft breeze was blowing across the grass runway, carrying with it the smell of aviation fuel. As they got closer, Jason could just make out the large shadows of the hangars. One by one, he searched the hangars until he found what he was looking for.

Back in the suburbs of London, a chauffeur-driven black Jaguar XJ6 stopped outside a home on Church Road. Police Commissioner John Lock stepped out. He rang the doorbell several times before the lights came on. Slowly the door opened. Dr. Turner, who was wearing a robe over his pajamas, looked out at the man in uniform.

"Yes?" he asked.

"Mr. Turner?" Lock asked.

"Well, it's Dr. Turner actually, but at midnight, it doesn't matter. Can I help you?"

"I need to speak to Scott. It's urgent," he said as he pushed the door back and walked in. "I know it's late, but I simply must talk to him."

"He's in bed and has school in the morning. But let me

guess. This has something to do with Jason?" Without invitation, Lock started walking up the stairs, followed by Dr. Turner and Mrs. Turner.

Scott was still asleep, lying on his side away from the door. Lock walked over, sat on the boy's bed, and woke Scott.

"Do you know who I am?"

"Yes, sir. You don't speak to me normally. Too important, but I've seen you at Scotland Yard Police Station.

"Then you know that I would only come here this late for a very important reason."

"Is Jason okay?"

"He's alive. I can tell you that. Did you see the news reports about the police station in Spain? That was the Triads. It looks like Jason and the girl got away. As you can imagine, the whole thing is a major embarrassment to the British government."

"Why?"

"We have an international incident on our hands! Over one hundred Spanish people have been killed—police and civilians. And it's not going to stop until the Triads get what they want."

"What do they want?" Dr. Turner asked.

"Simply, the girl as a hostage and Jason's dead body."

"Why are you telling me this now?" Scott asked.

"If on the odd chance Jason contacts you, you must warn him. He has to lie low and he must not trust anyone. I've said enough already, Scott. I was never here and we never had this conversation. Think on it. With Jason dead, they can close the case as a success. While he is still running around Europe, killing off his attackers, he is an embarrassment to the department."

"Are you serious? They are shooting at him. He's running for his life and *he's* an embarrassment?"

"Not to me, Scott. To me, Jason is a national treasure—a real hero. But every new body that turns up increases the pressure, and the prime minister wants it to stop and doesn't care how."

"Can't you give him any help?"

"I just did."

CHAPTER 26

THE HANGAR REVEALED THREE light aircraft. Jason smiled when he noticed a de Havilland Chipmunk, a small Canadian-made airplane. The two-seat training aircraft was the same model he had used for his pilot's license test. Jason made himself busy checking the fuel, battery, and controls. Joanne sat on a stack of tires and watched, somewhat surprised that Jason seemed to know what he was doing.

Jason finished checking the small aircraft. Joanne just stared in amazement as Jason started studying the maps he found inside the plane.

"So we hold a gun to a pilot's head now? I hope you noticed only two seats in the plane. You promised you would stay with me," Joanne anxiously said.

Jason turned and looked at her. She appeared much older now—her eyes set deeper and face thinner. She had witnessed too much for a young girl. He stopped what he was doing and put his arms around her and pulled her close. He gave her a peck on the cheek and they locked foreheads.

"Always look beyond what you can see," he quoted Wong Tong. "I don't break my promises, especially to those I—" He paused and went back to his maps.

"Those…you?"

"I'll fly it." He changed the subject.

"Jason, it's an aircraft, not a toy. You can't fly a plane."

"I can, and I'm going to as soon as it's light."

Joanne was not sure if he was joking, but she'd learned the hard way that anything was possible with Jason. She completely trusted him and would follow him anywhere.

As soon as dawn broke, Jason opened the large hangar doors. It took him a while to slide the huge doors back. His small body and weight had little impact on the large steel doors, but once he got them moving, they slid along quite easily. He walked outside and checked the windsock for wind direction. He looked his watch and went back over the aircraft checks. He was partially nervous about stealing a plane but also excited and wanted to show off his pilot skills to Joanne.

Joanne followed him and climbed up a small step to get into the backseat of the plane behind Jason.

He closed the roof and started the engine. The noise made Joanne jump. Slowly he released the brake and took the plane from the hangar. It bounced along the grass to the start of the runway. Jason turned the plane around and applied the brakes. He did a final check.

"Where are we going?" Joanne shouted above the engine noise.

"Over the top of them," he said, pointing to his right. "That's the Pyrenees Mountains and France. I want Spain to be far behind us."

Joanne looked at the snow-covered mountains in the distance and asked, "Is it safe to fly over them?" Joanne's nervous question was drowned out by the roar of the engine as Jason opened up the throttle. After a few seconds, he released the brakes, and they were rumbling down the runway. He opened the throttles up full, and when he had his required speed, he pulled the plane up into the morning sky.

The small plane soared across the sky heading northwest. He kept the plane lower than he should have as he was trying to hide from any radar. He also kept radio silence. Unfortunately they did encounter some heavy clouds and he was forced to fly higher.

As they flew over the French Pyrenees, heavy turbulence bounced the plane around—something he was not used to. It scared Joanne and Jason too, although he would never admit it. The scenery below them was breathtaking. Snowcapped mountains glistened in the morning sun. After just over an hour, the mountains got smaller and the land flatter. The turbulence finally settled and the flight became smooth again.

The plane broke through the clouds, and with her faced pressed against the window, Joanne suddenly saw the French countryside. With miniature houses and cars dotted around, the brilliant sunshine of the Spanish mainland had been replaced by the gray and uncertain weather of France.

"We're in France now," he shouted to Joanne. She was looking at the rich green fields below. Cows looked like dots, and the French farmhouses looked like toys. Jason checked his compass and tried looking at the map. After a few minutes, he gave up and threw the map over his shoulder.

"I'm lost."

"What about the map?"

"I've no idea where we are. I didn't follow a course. I just avoided the mountains. I'll just land somewhere. We don't have too much fuel anyway," he shouted back, unconcerned.

Joanne crossed her fingers as the plane banked and slowly started going down. Jason spotted a large field. It had trees at either end, but he was sure he could get low enough and land safely.

The plane's undercarriage missed the tops of the trees by just a few feet. Jason lowered it down and made a landing that was probably one of the best he had ever done. Once he turned the engine off, Joanne gave a sigh of relief. Jason was pleased with his first solo flight since he had gotten his pilot's license.

A few hundred yards away, he could see a farmhouse. He opened the roof of the cockpit and climbed out. They walked slowly toward the tiny farmhouse. A rooster was crowing. As they got closer, a man stepped out and raised his hand.

"*Bonjour!*" Jason shouted.

"*Bonjour!*" came a reply from the farmer, who crossed his arms, smiled, and shook his head. He was in his midforties with sand-colored hair and weather-beaten cheeks that suggested years spent outdoors.

"I have seen it all now. Children flying around the countryside to say good morning," he said in French.

"I'm afraid we're lost, sir. Do you have a telephone I can use?" Jason asked in French.

"This is Jason Steed. I need to speak to George Young."

Eventually an unfamiliar voice came on the phone.

"Jason, it's good to hear from you. I'm Simon Caldwell and currently running things here. George Young has taken a few days off. The stress of all this and his son's injuries. I'm sure you understand. Where are you?"

"France, just north of the Pyrenees in a village called Luz. We are at a small farm called Luz Orchard."

"Good. I'm glad you are safe. The girl, is she with you?"

"Yes, of course, she is. I'm not going to leave her. Now that we're out of Spain, can someone come and get us?"

"Yes, Jason. Stay where you are. I'll have someone there in a few hours. How did you get there?"

"I stole a plane. Will it be safe to come home yet?"

"Almost, Jason. We have one or two loose ends to tie up and then you will be coming home. Stay where you are. Soon it will be all over."

When Jason put down the phone, he felt uneasy. Something didn't seem right. It was too easy.

"May I use the phone again?" he asked the farmer. "I want to make sure they bring the correct fuel," Jason said.

He picked up the phone and dialed Scott's house.

"Hello," a familiar woman's voice answered.

"Mrs. Turner, it's Jason. I need to talk to Scott."

"Sorry, Jason. He's just left for school. Hang on. I can still see him. I will run out and call him." The phone line went quiet for a minute.

"Jase?"

"Scott?"

"It's good to hear your voice, mate. Where are you?"

"France."

"Wow, you sure get around. I'm glad you called. I need to talk to you." Scott explained everything—George's disappearance and the police commissioner's warning that Jason was not to trust anyone. "Jason, listen to me. I have this information from the highest authority—someone who cares about you. Whatever you do, don't trust anyone."

"Scott, I can trust SYUI."

"Jason. I'm serious. From now on, you trust no one. Oh, and one more thing."

"What?"

"Please look after yourself, mate. I miss you."

Five hours later, two black BMWs drove down the farm lane. Jason watched from the window as four men got out and one walked toward the farmhouse.

Jason went outside to meet him. He was a tall, slim man in his thirties, with short dark hair and watchful eyes. He wore jeans and a white shirt. Draped over his shoulders was a black leather jacket with a poppy in his buttonhole. It grabbed Jason's attention. Of course, it was November. It would soon be Remembrance Sunday, when the whole of England wore poppies and held a two-minute silence for those killed in the wars.

"Jason Steed? Whoa! They were right. You *are* just a kid. You flew in on that?" he said, pointing at the plane with his thumb.

"Yeah, and you are?" Jason asked.

"Patrick Thomas. We're with MI6. SYUI asked us to pick you up, as they don't have any agents in France. We were here on a mission anyway. Let's get going. We need to get you two safe as soon as possible."

Jason ran into the farmhouse and thanked the farmer and his wife. When he came back out, both cars had now moved down to the farmhouse. Joanne stuck by Jason's side. Something was wrong with what Patrick had just said to Jason. He could not put his finger on it, so he ignored it.

"Okay, Jason, you'll be riding with Jack and Trevor, and you, my pretty, will be riding with me and Tony."

"No, I'm going in the same car as Jason," Joanne argued.

"You'll be fine with us, love. Jason will be fine. We're all going to the same place, but it's harder for them to hit two cars. I can assure you we are professionals. We know what we are doing. Come along," Patrick said as he opened the back of the car. Joanne gave Jason a look and he picked up on it.

"Patrick, we go together," Jason said abruptly.

"No, Jason. Like I said, we need to make it harder for the Triad hit men."

"We've made it this far together. I managed to defend us myself. Now I have you *professionals* too. We should be doubly safe." Jason smirked as he climbed in the back of the car with Joanne. Patrick marched around to the other door and opened it.

"Jason, out. That's an order." He glared down at the boy.

"I don't take orders from MI6. If you've read my file, you know you can't physically force me out. I am *not* moving," Jason snapped. He snatched the door handle and pulled it shut.

Patrick cursed under his breath and waved the others away. As Patrick sat in the front passenger seat, he turned around and glared at the boy. "You just made my job a whole lot easier." He turned and faced the front before he said "Let's go." The two cars sped off, leaving the farmer with an aircraft in their field and no explanation.

Joanne put her hand on Jason's. He looked at her, and she gave a tight-lipped smile. She did not need to say anything. He knew she was grateful. Jason took her hand and sat in deep thought. He raised his hand to his forehead and rubbed his head.

Don't trust anyone, Scott said. You just made my job a whole lot easier, Patrick said. No, Patrick is MI6. He wouldn't hurt us.

He tried to piece together the puzzle. His instincts were telling him something was wrong.

The poppy. They don't wear them in France. Patrick said he was here in France anyway. Why would he be wearing a poppy? Unless he lied and just flew over from the United Kingdom. Why would he lie to me?

"Patrick, are we going to meet George Young?" Jason asked.

Patrick looked across at the driver who paused and turned around. "Oh, yes. Soon this will be all over for you. You'll meet George Young real soon." He gave a smirk and turned back around. The driver looked at Patrick. Jason could see in the mirror that the driver almost laughed at the remark. He took Joanne's hand out of his right one and placed it on his leg. She looked at him, and he looked back without speaking. He looked at Patrick and silently mouthed the word "Shush." She immediately understood and kept quiet. Slowly he put his hand down the front of his pants and found the gun. He gently pulled it out and flicked the safety switch off.

CHAPTER 27

They had been driving north for two hours before they turned off the main road. They followed the other car down a small lane. When they came across a large wooded area, the front car stopped in a clearing.

"Why are we stopping here?" Jason asked, concerned.

"It's a safe place where we can stretch our legs. We have a long way to go, and I'm sure you need a bathroom break," Patrick replied.

"I'm fine," Joanne said.

"So you do speak. Well, stretch your legs anyway."

Jason was not sure if he had read the situation right or not. It was a safe place to stop after all. He moved closer to Joanne and put his right hand and gun behind her back. He lifted the back of her cardigan and forced the gun into the back of her shorts. She didn't question it and positioned herself to allow Jason access. Once it was secure, he pulled her cardigan over the back of her shorts.

Patrick climbed out. Jason opened his door, climbed out, and made sure Joanne came with him. Once outside, he put his arm around her waist. The other agents stood by their car and watched Patrick and the driver, but nothing was said. A large cloud covered the sun and cast a dark shadow and deadly silence. Jason's nerves were tingling.

"You look like a couple of young lovers. Is he your boyfriend?"

asked the driver. Joanne forced a smile but made no comment. Trevor opened the trunk of his car. He put his hand in and lifted what looked like the handle of a shovel and then put it back after he looked at Patrick. Jason moved his hand under the back of Joanne's cardigan and found the gun. Slowly he pulled it out from the back of her shorts and found the trigger with his finger. He moved it up her back and kept it hidden by her cardigan.

These guys are MI6. I can't afford to miss.

Patrick put his back to them and took something out of his pocket. Before Jason could move, the man turned and pointed a gun at them.

"Sorry, kids. We're following orders. You did a good job, but now it's a bloody mess. The powers that be want it cleaned up and quick. There is a general election in three weeks, and it's too close to call. Jason, once you join George Young and we hand the girl over to the Chinese, it will end," Patrick said. The driver took the shovel out of the trunk, and without showing any emotion, he stuck it in the ground and started digging a grave.

"My dad will get you for this!" Joanne shouted.

"No, he won't. He'll just be pleased to have you back."

"But you could be passing her over to the Triads," Jason pleaded.

"No, give us some credit. They will send another agent to collect her. The last guy, one of their top secret agents, was killed outside the police station," Patrick spoke calmly and kept the gun pointed at Jason.

The man in white, Jason thought.

Jason kept his hand and gun underneath her cardigan. She turned and hugged him, crying out loud, her back to Patrick. Jason concentrated, ready to make his move.

"Any last requests?" Jason asked.

"No, you don't get any, son," he said.

"Actually, I was asking you." Jason aimed the gun and fired at Patrick twice. The bullets went through Joanne's cardigan and hit the target. Jason put his right foot behind Joanne's legs and pushed her over onto the ground. As she fell, he opened fire on the driver, and the bullet went directly into his chest and pierced his heart. Out of the corner of his eye, Jason noticed the other two agents taking their guns out of their jackets. He dove to the ground and fired at them. One was hit in the chest. The other jumped over the front of their car and fired back.

Jason crawled along the gravel and hid behind Patrick's body. He took aim at the agent's car but was out of bullets. He scrambled along the ground for Patrick's gun. A flurry of bullets pounded the body of Patrick and gravel all around Jason. The gunfire ceased. Jason peered over Patrick's body and noticed the agent was crawling behind the car.

He's out of bullets too!

Jason ran toward the car and then dove on the ground. When he looked under the car, he could see the man trying to crawl away. Jason opened fire, shooting the underside of the car and catching the fuel tank. A large ball of flame shot out from the back of the car, eventually engulfing the whole car in flames. Jason rolled away from the growing heat. The MI6 agent started screaming as his clothing caught fire. Jason ran and pulled him away from the burning car, rolling him over in the process. His Sea Cadet first aid training became useful.

Once he was clear, he ran back to check on Joanne. She sat up and looked at the two holes in the back of her cardigan.

"Are you all right?" Jason asked.

She nodded.

He helped her up and then walked over to the surviving agent. He was lying on his back and holding his chest wound. The skin on the back of his hands and one side of his face was burned, swollen, and seeping.

"Why? Why did you save me?" he groaned.

"I may still kill you. I may put you through a lot of pain first. Or I may take you to a hospital. I know what you would prefer, but in return, you have to talk to me. We're on the same side."

"They were good agents, good men, and good friends."

"If they are so good, why would you want to kill me? What did I do wrong?" Jason shouted.

"What Patrick told you. You did a great job uncovering Boudica's operation. But she got away and you stirred up a hornet's nest. The Triads will stop at nothing. The amount of people killed in Spain was nothing short of a massacre. The Spanish authorities have put a huge amount of pressure on the British government. With you out of the way, everything can settle down before the election."

Jason sat down next to Trevor and put his head between his knees, trying to think. It was a shock to learn that he was not only hunted by the Triads and the Spanish police but his own country.

"What can I do? I can't run forever. How can it be stopped?"

Feeling betrayed by his own country, his voice started breaking and his eyes welled up.

The agent studied Jason. The poor kid was scared to death and way out of his depth. He felt sorry for him. "You should have taken out Boudica. We know the Triads are gathering somewhere here in France, but we're not sure where. We think George Young knew, but he's now probably at the bottom of the River Thames. You'll just have to keep running and hide." Trevor groaned in pain.

"Who gave the order to kill me?"

"Jason, I can't say that."

"I need to know."

"It doesn't matter. I can't tell you. That's one thing I will never do—betray my superior officers."

"You would rather die?"

"Yes," the man said.

Jason looked at him. He admired his loyalty.

"You just lost your trip to the hospital, but I will call and get you help." He picked himself up and walked back over to Joanne.

"Can you drive?" he asked.

"No, but I am sure you can."

"Actually, I can't." Jason looked a little embarrassed. "But it's an automatic car, so it should be simple." He took the wallets from all the MI6 agents so he'd have money. He sat in the front of the car and pulled the driver's seat as far forward as it would go. He could just reach the brake and throttle. He found a road map and studied it.

"Buckle up. Let's go."

"Where?"

"Mont Blanc. George Young mentioned it to me. He told me he would love to be able to go to Mont Blanc in France and get Boudica. I think that's where the Triads are meeting."

"Jason, that's the last place in the world we want to be," she gasped.

"No…it's the last place they would expect us to be. It's the only place to find Boudica and end this."

CHAPTER 28

JASON GINGERLY DROVE THE car a few feet and slowly turned around and then drove back down the lane. Once on the main road, he found it hard to go the same speed as the other cars. He sat as close to the wheel as he could. He was surprised to find it was actually hard to drive.

"We are drawing attention, Jason. Go faster." With his knuckles white with the tight grip he had on the steering wheel, he slowly increased his speed to be the same as the other cars. "Jason, you're too close to the edge. Keep over a bit," she said, trying to move away from the side of the car. Eventually he got used to it and could relax slightly.

After seven hours driving with the occasional stop for fuel and snacks, they stopped at a truck stop, found a quiet corner, and parked for the night. They slept in the back together and woke cold and hungry early in the morning. Jason drove for another four hours until the road ran parallel to the French and Italian border. He started to enjoy the drive. His car was powerful and responsive. The tinted windows help prevent other drivers getting a good look at him and his age.

Eventually the huge, snow-covered mountains and Mont Blanc, the largest of them all, poked out of the low clouds. The village of Saint-Gervais-les-Bains was a ski resort. It was early November, and although cold and covered with snow, the heavy snows had not yet fallen. Within a month, the village would come alive with skiers from around the world.

They went to the center of activity, a small café, and spoke to some of the local people. He invented a story that he and his stepsister were with their parents, who were looking to buy a lodge in the area. He said that they had gotten bored and had come to the village. They joined two elderly men who sat outside. They welcomed the young strangers, especially when Jason bought them both a fresh coffee. Joanne looked up at the surrounding mountains. The village was in a valley, and it was just starting to get its winter cloak of snow. Above, the great purple-blue mountains poked out above the clouds—their flanks gleaming with swathes of white.

"We found a lady's ring. I think I saw a Chinese lady drop it. I would love to return it. We may get a reward," Jason explained. "The lady was Chinese with blond hair. She had white skin and red lipstick. She kinda looked like a doll."

Pierre, a retired mechanic, took a sip from his coffee and nodded. "Yes, there was such a lady here last week at the butcher's. I'm sure it's a wig, not her hair. The Chinese do not have your color hair. The butcher says she bought a huge amount of fresh meat and paid cash. There are hundreds of Chinese here staying at the castle. I have heard it said that she owns it. I'm sure she would give you children a reward if you have found her ring."

Jason thanked them and left with Joanne.

They walked across the street and looked up at the castle. It was half-built into the side of the mountain about four hundred feet from the ground. A small road meandered its way up to the castle. It was just large enough for a small car. They went into a ski supply store. Jason purchased rope, binoculars, a knife, and some climbing gloves.

"How much money do we have left?" Joanne asked.

"More than enough. I haven't even started on Patrick's money yet."

"Can we get a hotel room? I would love to take a shower." Jason looked at her and smiled. Her hair was tangled after sleeping in the car the night before, and neither of them had washed for three days. He nodded at her.

They chose the Hotel de Mar, a small three-story hotel with a steeply sloped roof. As they entered the hall, it seemed quite small on the inside and cold. A young woman was on the telephone taking a reservation. Patiently, they waited, looking around the inside.

"Can I help you?" she asked in French.

"Our father has asked us to book a room. He has to drive back to the airport. We left some of our luggage there. We'd like a room on the top floor overlooking the square if you have one please," Jason said in French.

"You have no reservations?"

"No, but he gave me his credit card," Jason said and passed Patrick's credit card.

"That will do nicely. I have a family room on the top floor. It can sleep six. How long are you staying?"

"I don't know. Father works and drags us all over the world with him. I am sure it will be a few days."

They were given a key with a very large plastic key fob attached.

Joanne ran to the bathroom and immediately started to run the bath. She emptied all the shampoo into the tub to make as many bubbles as she could. Jason looked out the window and studied the castle with the binoculars.

"Jason. Come in here." Joanne's voice strained from inside the bathroom. He approached and slowly opened the door.

"Is it all right to come in?" he asked as he noticed her clothing spread across the floor.

"Yes."

He cautiously looked through the steam-filled room to the huge bathtub. Frothy white bubbles spilled over the sides and up the back wall. Among the bubbles was Joanne, with just her head showing. He laughed when he saw her.

"Get in." She laughed.

Jason blushed. "No. I'll wait until you finish."

"Don't be a baby. Get in. It's big enough for both of us. I promise I won't look."

He wiped the condensation off the mirror and looked at himself. He was dirty and tired. His whole body ached. He looked back at Joanne, and a large grin spread across his face.

"Don't you dare look!" he laughed.

In a flash, he was undressed and sitting at the other end of the tub consumed by bubbles. "How much stuff did you put in? I'll smell like flowers after this."

"All of it," she said, laughing as she threw a handful of soap suds at him. He threw some back. She made a bubble beard for him and called him Santa Claus.

For a few moments, they could enjoy being children, tickling each other's feet, slipping beneath the sea of bubbles, coming up laughing, and blowing the suds away. They forgot about the death they had witnessed and the trouble that lay ahead. Jason felt strangely at peace.

Jason put the room's telephone to use. He called SYUI and asked to speak to Simon Caldwell. He was in a meeting, but as soon as Jason gave his name, he was put directly through.

"Hello?"

"I…the four MI6 agents you sent to kill me—one of them was alive when I left, but the other three are dead. Don't send any more. I don't enjoy hurting our own people."

There was a long silence.

"Jason, it's not like it seems. It's complicated," Caldwell replied.

"When this is all over," Jason said and then paused, his voice breaking with emotion. "When this is all over, I'm coming to get *you*."

He stood for a moment, looking at the phone and tapping the receiver. He wanted to call his father, but he knew his dad would just order him home. But he couldn't leave until Boudica was caught.

After a few hours, they ordered room service and Jason continued to study the castle. He watched as more people arrived. If his plan was going to work, he had to wait for the right moment. Then he saw her. Her blond wig cut into a straight bob. Her expressionless face—it was Boudica.

"You bitch," Jason said, cursing at the same time. He gritted his teeth and squinted his eyes.

"What did I do?" Joanne asked.

"Not *you*. Come and look. I think it's Boudica. It's hard to say for sure. She is too far away to get a good look."

Joanne looked through the binoculars and said, "Where?"

"To the left of the castle. Look at the large balcony. The woman with the blond hair."

Joanne searched with the binoculars. "I see her. Can we call SYUI now? She is playing with a dog or something. She's petting something and feeding it."

Jason took the binoculars off her and looked. Boudica was walking up and down. The balcony covered everything from her waist down, so it was impossible to see the dog.

"I have to be sure it's her before I call. I have to get ready. It'll be dark soon. I know I said I wouldn't leave you, but you can't come with me. Stay here and I'll find out if it's her and then call SYUI."

"Promise me you will come back, Jason."

"I promise."

He put the gun in his pocket, clipped the knife to his belt, and put the rope over his shoulder. Before he left, he walked over to Joanne and bent forward to kiss her good-bye. She turned and kissed him on his lips. He slowly pulled away a few inches. They gazed into each other's eyes and smiled.

"I promise," he said. "I will be back."

Then she was alone.

CHAPTER 29

THE COLD NIGHT AIR soon brought him to his senses. He had a job to do. He had no plan of action—just a desire to finish this once and for all.

He walked across the courtyard and started walking up the single-track road, his feet crunching on some newly laid snow. He walked as close to the castle as he could without being seen. There was a sliver of a crescent moon and a sky full of stars. But away from the streetlights, he was engulfed by silence and darkness. The old castle cast a dark, gloomy shadow. It was like stepping back a thousand years in time. The once-busy town square was deserted and silent. It gave Jason a chill. His heartbeat was echoing in his ears. The regular thud was the only sound.

Just before the castle, a cold mist hung in the air. The road was dimly lit. He could see two guards standing outside. They clapped their hands together and stamped their feet, trying to keep warm. Their breaths formed billowing clouds of steam. He left the road and walked gingerly along the side of the steep bank. He paused and listened. He thought he heard something in the darkness behind him—a shuffling noise.

It didn't take him long to reach the edge of the mountain wall. An owl hooted just above his head and made him jump. He told himself to calm down, but then he heard it again. He was convinced something was following and shuffling close behind him. His heart raced, and his feet seemed frozen to the spot. He took a deep breath and stood in a fighting stance, ready to take on his pursuer. His eyes strained in the darkness, trying to see what was approaching.

The shuffling noise continued to get closer. He screamed when he felt something heavy brush against his leg. It was a marmot—a ratlike creature the size of a dog. It ran off as soon as it heard Jason scream.

"Stupid animal," he cursed under his breath.

Jason tried to calm himself down and then smiled to himself for being so stupid.

A solitary guard stood at the side of the castle and he stopped to light a cigarette. Jason knew this was a perfect chance to strike. As he crept up on the man, he lashed out with his right leg, pivoting on his hip. With a faint groan, the guard clattered to the ground and didn't get up.

"See, smoking's bad for your health," Jason snickered.

He slowly started climbing up the rock face. His eyes grew accustomed to the darkness, and the moonlight gave just enough light. As he made his way up the steep bank, he stopped at the brickwork of the castle. There were no handrails or footholds here. He had to lie as flat as he could and clamber up. He noticed a set of large bricks on the edge of the castle's base protruding out. With one hand, he made a lasso and threw it up to the protruding bricks. It took him four attempts to catch a brick. Once he did, he pulled it tight and slowly walked up the wall, hand over hand. It seemed to take a lot longer than he had thought. As he neared the top, he pulled himself up.

He came to the lower level of the castle. He looked up. It was a long way to go before getting to the balcony. The castle wall was built of heavy granite bricks that were rough and slightly rounded. Jason started climbing. Using his fingers and lying flat against the brickwork, he slowly climbed up. His shoes gave no grip, so he kicked them off along with his socks and carried on up barefoot. His small toes dug into the crevices for support. His small, lightweight, but strong body was perfect for climbing. An adult would not have been able to scale the building so easily.

It was a long, tiring climb. His toes started to ache and scratch on the rough surface. When he was over forty feet up, he noticed that the wall was getting damp and slippery. Relentlessly, he carried on, breathing deeply as he exhausted his body's strength. Now over halfway and one hundred feet up, his body was tired, but he could not go back down. He had to keep going.

Not one of your best ideas, was it?

He concentrated and tried to ignore the pain in his hands and feet—all the time wishing he was back in the warm hotel room with Joanne. He had no idea how he would call for help once he confirmed seeing Boudica.

He looked up and realized he was close. It gave him new life and he pulled and pushed his body up. Once he got a grip on the top wall of the balcony, he pulled himself over onto Boudica's balcony. He stopped to catch his breath and take in his surroundings.

The balcony was long with a metal table and chairs in the center. It had a large, black, arch-shaped door that entered into the castle. He assumed it was Boudica's room. The balcony stretched around the corner. At the back was a steep drop into the darkness. He slowly walked across to the doorway and stopped as he put his bare foot on something soft. Immediately the stench hit his senses. It was animal droppings.

He made a face and wiped his foot across the floor and then made his way to the doorway. He slowly turned the iron handle and opened the door a crack. Light escaped from inside. Quickly, he opened the door and stepped in.

It was the most magnificent bedroom he had ever seen. It was better than anything he had seen at Buckingham Palace while he was visiting Princess Catherine. Boudica sat on a four-poster bed, reading. Behind the bed was a floor-to-ceiling mirror in a decorated gold frame. She looked up and then looked back down at her book as if he were insignificant. All the furniture was antique and would not have looked out of place in a museum. In the center of the room, a large chandelier with six curving arms hung, its crystal teardrops shining like diamonds, dancing light around the room.

Boudica was stunning. There was no other way for Jason to describe her. She was more like a film star than a criminal. Her blond wig was perfectly cut. She smiled and tilted her head and looked at him.

"Jason, darling, you are full of surprises. I would never in a million years have expected to see you here." She turned the corner of the page she was reading and calmly put the book down. "There. It's a good book—I don't wish to lose my page." Jason was squinting, trying to get his eyes accustomed to the light.

"Can I get you something to drink?"

"Your blood would be nice."

"Darling, there is no need for that here. You are remarkable. You've taken out some of the best hit men we have. Now look at you. You scale the walls of my castle—truly amazing. You would be very valuable to our organization. Look around you. We have more money than you could ever have imagined. It could all be yours one day." She lifted a silver jug and poured water into a gleaming crystal glass.

"Have some water," she said and offered Jason the glass.

"You are sicker than I thought if you think I would join your organization." He smiled meanly. "Besides, most of it is gone," he said as he took the water.

"Tomorrow the Triad leaders hold a meeting. Once I have my assets back in China—with the help of the girl—all will be fine. Then we can put the money to good use. Chairman Mao will no longer rule China, and I will have my revenge…on you." She threw back her head and laughed. Her blond hair looked more out of place on her oriental face.

"Shame you won't be around to join them. Where is George Young?" Jason was now next to her bed, standing on his toes, his fists clenched.

"Jason, darling, calm down. You and I are so much alike. We would make a great team. I have always wanted a son." Her voice was soft and very precise.

Jason drank his water and threw the glass against the wall. "Funny that. I've always wanted a mother, but I'd rather be dead than have a mother like you. Now, where is George or do I have to beat it out of you like you did to Jim Kinver?"

Boudica's smile turned to a frown. She raised her hand and admired her long fingernails. "Then you shall have your wish and die. Have you met Luke, Jason? I'm sure he will like you. He loved your old friend, Andrew. Luke, come here, boy." A deep growl came from a closet, and Luke, the leopard, stepped out and stared at the boy. Jason took a deep breath.

"Yes, he seems to like you too. You know he ate Andrew in just two days. You are smaller, so I doubt it will take him so long with you."

Jason backed away but kept his eyes on Luke, who was getting closer, crouching down as he stalked him. Boudica crossed her legs and smiled as she rubbed her hands together. Luke's yellow eyes were now fixed on him, and he could almost hear the leopard's only thought: *Fresh food.* Jason was not sure how much a leopard could eat but was pretty sure there wouldn't be a great deal left.

"Luke…kill."

The leopard growled. It was a low-pitch rumbling noise that came deep from within its body. It was one of the most terrifying noises Jason had ever heard. Without a second's notice, Luke's yellow eyes darkened, and he pounced. Its open jaw revealed huge white fangs. Jason saw the perfect muscles rippling beneath the fur. He had to defend himself the only way he knew how.

Every karate instructor he had ever had had told him he was the fastest they had seen. His reactions were faster than any opponent he had come across. But was he faster than a leopard?

As the gaping jaws got closer, he instinctively blocked with his left forearm, which smashed against the side of Luke's face and kept the fatal fangs away from his throat. He grabbed his knife with his right hand. Luke's large claws ripped into Jason's arm. Jason's left hand grabbed at Luke's neck in an effort to avoid its mouth. They both fell then—Jason on his back. Luke's back legs started clawing and gouging at Jason's thigh. Jason screamed out in pain. He then plunged his knife into Luke's back.

Luke gave an ear-shattering roar. His front paw and claws swiped across Jason's face, just missing his eyes. Jason's soft skin was ripped open with such ease. He knew he had to act quickly before Luke literally tore him apart. Again, Jason plunged the knife into Luke a second time, this time as deep as he could. Luke leapt off Jason and circled him, growling loudly and in pain. Jason was pumped with adrenaline. He jumped to his feet—his pupils dilated. He was now in survival mode and at his most lethal.

This time, Jason attacked Luke and screamed at the top of his lungs. The knife cut into Luke's neck. The leopard was taken by surprise and tried to retreat, but Jason struck again. He swung wildly at Luke, who was now cowering away, blood running down his coat. Out of the corner of his eye, Jason noticed Boudica had slipped off the bed and was trying to get away. Jason leapt onto the bed, bounced off the other side, and kicked out at Boudica. To his surprise, she blocked his kick and counterattacked with a fist. Jason blocked with his forearm and landed on his feet.

"What have you done to Luke? You despicable boy, you have no idea what this is all about. You pathetic child, this is bigger than you and your George Young ever dreamed of. I'm about to change history."

Jason ignored her and threw out a full roundhouse kick. She went to block the kick; however, it was just a feint. Jason quickly pulled back and then struck out a second time, catching her in the stomach. She was knocked against the wall.

"You will die for this! You will suffer a very slow and painful death. There are people in very high places who are counting on me." She coughed, pushing away from the wall. Suddenly, she ran screaming at Jason. He caught her hands, but her momentum and body weight pushed him back. He stepped back, trying to keep his balance, until he eventually tripped over the doorstep. He fell on his back—her on top of him. Boudica head-butted his face, and Jason's nose broke. He cried out in pain as blood covered his cheeks and mouth. She sank her teeth into his neck and tore at his skin. Pain shot through his body. He had dropped his knife in the fall, but he used all his strength to push her off.

Once he forced her off, he rolled across the balcony and put a hand on his neck wound. She picked up his knife and circled him, panting like a wild animal. She smiled and licked his blood off her chin. Jason was fighting to stay conscious, and he started feeling light-headed.

Concentrate. Don't lose it now. Wake up.

"It's time for you to die, Jason Steed. Your stupid attempt to stop me has done nothing but slow things down. You really have no idea what this is all about, do you?" She said and grinned.

"Yes," he said. "Greed. You want everyone addicted to your cereal so you can increase the price and make a fortune. Then bribe people in China to take over the government." Jason was hurt. He was angry with himself for getting injured and annoyed he was being laughed at.

She laughed again and then attacked him. It seemed like slow motion to Jason. Her attack was predictable. She raised her knife arm and ran forward. He turned, bent his legs slightly, and caught her arm as it came down. He pulled down hard on her arm, using her own body weight against her, and performed a basic judo throw. She was launched onto the back wall, which stood waist high. Her body slumped over the edge, her legs kicking out, trying to counterbalance her weight. He grabbed her ankle and pushed it up, holding her balanced on the wall.

"Now, tell me where George Young is or you'll need to learn to fly!" he panted.

She cursed at him. "Let me go, you little horror." More curse words followed in English and Chinese.

Enraged and high on adrenaline, he did just what she asked. "Okay."

CHAPTER 30

As Jason released his grip, Boudica's body slid over the wall. She fell silently to her death. He looked over the wall and waited. After a few seconds, he heard a faint thud several hundred feet below.

He staggered back into her room and then into her bathroom. He regretted letting her go. He knew he should have found out where George was first. The cold water applied to his nose slowed the bleeding. He noticed the skin around his eyes was already turning black. He bled from his face, arms, hands, and thigh. His neck had teeth marks from her bite. He felt cheated by Boudica's death. He had expected more.

Luke growled at him but didn't come out from his hiding place. Jason went outside and looked over the wall. He was too exhausted to climb down. With his injuries, he would probably fall to his death.

He pulled the gun out of his pants and opened her bedroom door. It led to a long corridor with cream carpet. The walls were covered in red silk, and imitation flame lights lit up the entire corridor. He slowly walked along, gun in one hand and a blood-stained cloth over his nose with the other.

He heard voices and tried to discover if they were coming from in front of him or behind him. He was having difficulty correctly focusing. He put the gun back in his pants and kept walking. Ahead, he noticed three approaching men wearing the same black clothing. They looked puzzled when they saw Jason. He nodded and kept moving.

"What happened to you, boy?" one asked in Chinese.

"I fell," he replied but kept walking.

"Wait. Why have you no shoes? Who are you?" he asked.

Jason ignored him and kept walking. He could see some stairs ahead but could hear footsteps behind him. The men were getting closer.

"Stop. Who are you?" they shouted. Jason stopped and cursed at the man. He was too tired to fight. He pulled out the gun and shot him. The other two men tried to turn and run, but Jason opened fire and cut them both down. An alarm sounded across the entire castle. Jason made it to the stairs and started running down two at a time. After a few floors, he tripped, fell, rolled down some stairs, and dropped the gun in the chaos. He looked up and could not focus correctly. His broken nose and injuries had put his body into shock.

Not now. Wake up.

He staggered to his feet and walked down a corridor, holding onto a wall for support, leaving a blood-stained trail. He opened a door and searched for a hiding place. Inside, two men sat playing cards. They jumped up and shouted. He darted out and went back to the stairs. They now gave chase, and after a few more steps, they were right on his tail. He felt a hand grab his arm. Jason swung around, grabbed the arm, and brought his knee down, breaking the man's arm. The second man kicked Jason, catching the boy in the chest. Jason fell back into a fire extinguisher and landed on the ground.

Three others arrived and circled him. Jason jumped to his feet and attacked them, switching from one leg to another, kicking out at anything that moved. As he jumped from one foot to the next, his body working automatically—his mind was blank. One by one, they were knocked down and then he made his way down more flights of steps. Even more gave chase. As he rounded a corner, he noticed at least six men running up the stairs. He was surrounded and completely exhausted.

Jason could hear someone grunting and realized it was him. Every movement was an effort—fighting to breath, gasping for air, forcing himself not to give up. He took off down the corridor, but after a few paces, he noticed more men ahead of him. He was trapped. He ran at them, and while he stood on one leg and kicked out to keep them back, he fumbled for the handle on a door to his left. Fortunately, it wasn't locked. He jumped in and locked it.

Immediately his followers turned the handle and started banging on the door. He took in his surroundings. He was in a bedroom. It was modern and looked just like a hotel room. A man's clothing was set out on the dresser. Steam and the sound of running water came from the bathroom. The banging got louder on the door while Jason frantically looked for a way out. He found a jug of water on a tray, calmly took a drink, and poured the rest over his head, trying to wake himself up. He ran to the narrow, stained-glass window, opened it, and looked down.

He was still nearly a hundred feet up and could not risk climbing down. He noticed a large power cable a few feet below his window. It was dark outside, and he could not see where it went; however, it angled down and away from the castle.

The water from the shower stopped, and the banging grew louder. They were now using a fire extinguisher against the door, which shook with every bang. It would not hold them for much longer. He was exhausted and out of options.

"What's going on?" a naked Chinese man shouted when he came out of the shower.

Jason picked the man's pants off the dresser, wrapped the lower part of a leg around his left hand, and jumped up on the windowsill. The man ran to the door to open it, and Jason launched himself at the cable.

Please hold my weight.

He grabbed the cable and swung. Then he lifted his legs and hooked one of his legs onto the cable for support. It was a lot thicker than he had thought, and it was wet. He hooked the other pant leg over the cable and rolled his right hand around it. The pants were now hanging with a leg on either side of the cable, and he had a pant leg in each of his hands. The cold night air on his wet face and hair brought Jason back to life and gave him the will to live.

"Shoot him quick. He is getting a way!" a voice from the window shouted.

Jason released his legs and swung forward and started sliding down the cable. His speed soon increased. He knew it would come to a sudden stop eventually, but he did not know where exactly. But with gunshots coming from behind, he did not really care. He lifted his feet out in front of him to break his fall. It was dark, but the moon gave enough light to see a large electric tower approaching fast.

His homemade sling stopped at a large insulator a few feet from the tower. He was thrown up into the air, swinging six feet away from the tower. He thought about swinging back and forth and trying to grab the tower with his feet, but the heavy hum of electricity told him that was a bad idea. If he touched the electrified tower while he was holding the pants and cable, he could get cooked by the current. He swung back and forth and let go. For a few brief seconds, he was falling—that is, until he grabbed the metal crossbar on the tower.

"Ouch," he cursed as his forearm smashed against the cold metal.

Immediately he started to climb down. Behind him, he could hear shouting from the castle. Boudica's men started to swarm outside with flashlights. Jason dropped a section at a time, jumped the last twenty feet, and rolled free. He got to his feet and started running through the small area of grassland. He leapt over a gate and was now on the hard road surface. His bare feet made no sound as they sprinted across the courtyard toward the hotel among the parked cars. He ran up the steps and burst through the doors. He briefly stopped and looked back to ensure he had not been followed and then ran through the hotel lobby and pounded up the stairs.

He knocked on his door and waited patiently, panting as sweat ran down his blood-covered face. What was left of his shirt was stuck to his body. When the door opened, he darted inside and quickly closed the door behind him. His nose was swollen and bent to one side. His eyes were dark, and his tear ducts were working overtime.

"Jason? Oh no! What happened? Look at you," Joanne cried

as she tried to put her arms around him. He pushed her away and walked toward a table that had a half-full bottle of Coke. He struggled to drink it between heavy breaths. Joanne studied him and his horrific wounds. She put a hand on his arm, trying to comfort him, but he winced in pain and moved away.

"Let me call an ambulance," she said.

Jason planted an evil look on her while he continued to drink. The last thing he could do was get the local authorities involved.

"Well, I don't know what to do, Jason. You need to clean the wounds. I'll run a bath." She disappeared into the bathroom and turned on the water, but when she reappeared, she found Jason sitting on the edge of the bed with his head down. He felt faint and sick. His head was spinning, and every part of his body was sore. "What happened, Jason?"

"She didn't want to hang around, so I let her go."

"But look at your face. Your eyes are black. Your nose—it's out of shape. It looks like a boxer's nose."

"Thanks," he said.

"And it's all cut."

"She had a pet leopard. Luke, I think she called it. It was huge and crazy. It attacked me." He painfully lifted his arm and looked at the scratches.

"Are you sure you're okay? You look like you're seeing stars."

"Stars? I can see a whole galaxy. I'll be okay," he sighed.

"Where are your shoes and socks? Oh, Jason…your leg is cut open too." She bent down and looked at his leg. He lay back on the bed, his body still shaking from shock, exhaustion, or the cold—he was not sure. He closed his eyes.

"Come on. Get clean and then you can sleep. You don't want an infection." She pulled his hand and got him to his feet. He was in a haze. His head throbbed. He never complained when she undressed him and bathed him. Small matters like being in the state of undress did not seem important now. After a bath, she put him to bed. He remembered nothing more until the morning.

He was woken by the knock on the door.

"Room service," a woman's voice called. Joanne jumped up and greeted the woman and took the tray of plates covered with polished, stainless steel covers—a large jug of orange juice, cereals, and a newspaper.

Jason rolled over. He blinked several times to clear his vision. He looked at his watch and blinked again. He groaned as his body ached with every move he made. His nose and face were tender to the touch.

"Morning, sleepy. How are you feeling?" she asked, pouring the orange juice into the glasses.

"Thirsty and like I have been hit by a train and dragged along the track." He held out his hand and looked at the grazes on his knuckles. "You see this thumb?" He held his thumb out, and Joanne came to look at it.

"Yes," she said.

"Well, that's the only thing that doesn't hurt." He grinned.

"Get up and eat something. You'll feel better. You don't have much clothing left again," she sighed. "I'll go out after breakfast to the store across the road and get you some new clothes and shoes. What size shoes do you wear?" she asked as she passed him some juice.

When Joanne returned with the clothes, Jason put them on and looked at himself in the mirror.

"I look like a panda," he said, looking at his swollen nose and two very dark black eyes.

"I have never seen anyone with two black eyes before. Your nose is still pretty swollen too. It looks dented."

"I'm certain it's broken. It hurts like hell. My friend's dad is a plastic surgeon. He'll fix it for me. He covered up two bullet wounds for me once."

"You've been shot before?" She looked at him with her mouth open.

"Yeah, that hurt like hell too. I don't want to get shot again. I think I should call SYUI now."

A knock came on the door. "Room service." Jason looked at her, concerned.

"I didn't order anything more," he shouted back at the door.

"I have come to collect your tray, sir," the voice from behind the door called. Joanne went and opened the door. A woman in a maid's outfit entered and headed toward the tray. She stared at Jason and his face. He turned away and looked out the window up at the castle. It seemed quiet now. The Triads must have given up the search for him. People were busy in the street below going from store to store. He could just see the café on the corner, and he noticed the same old men sitting around the tables, drinking coffee. Jason picked up the phone to call SYUI.

"Ouch." He felt a sharp pain in his back. He quickly turned around and saw Joanne being carried out of the room. Two men in the familiar black clothing had grabbed her and covered her mouth. Two other men watched Jason. One was lowering a gun. Jason put his hand behind his back and felt something sticking out. He pulled it out and looked at it. In his hand was a tranquilizer dart.

"Let her go!" he shouted and tried to move forward, but his legs felt like lead—almost as if they were stuck to the floor. His right knee gave way first, and he fell forward onto his hands. "Let her go! Joanne!" He fought against the oncoming sleep and tried to stand. He was dizzy. The room seemed to be at an angle. His head was turning, trying to keep focus. His mind went blank— and then darkness.

CHAPTER 31

TRIAD LEADERS FROM AROUND the world met as planned in the grand hall of the castle. A long, polished cherry wood table was set on a raised stage at one end. At the table sat the Triad Dragon leaders. Eleven of the most evil men sat together for the very first time. A seat near the center was empty. The nameplate on the table read "Boudica."

Below the stage and twenty feet back were row upon row of seats filled with Triads deputy leaders, Triad vanguards, and Triad Red pole members. The vanguards were the operation officers, and the Red poles the enforcers.

The meeting was arranged by Boudica to regroup and stop the breakup of the Triads. However, not every Triad group was behind her. Many felt that Boudica had gone too far. Many of their own children and grandchildren had also been addicted to Coca-Bites.

The Dragon head, Chun Low, started to speak. He was in his midsixties, with a bald head. He had a scar across his face from his left eye to his mouth. It was an old injury from a fight when he was in his twenties.

"Welcome to the meeting. We all know why we are here. Some of you may not know that Boudica has not been seen since last night when we were raided. Well, I am pleased to inform you we have the parties responsible in our custody, and we will deal with them here and now. As you are aware, over sixty of our brave men fought in honor of our sacred traditions and oaths. Fought and died." He paused, his voice shaking in anger before he carried on. "Bring them out!"

An overweight man was marched out to the floor in front of the stage. He was handcuffed and had a sack over his head. He was pushed down to kneel before the stage. The sack was removed. George squinted as the bright light hit his eyes. His greasy hair was stuck up in all directions. He was unshaven and sweating. He looked around the room at his captors.

A girl was marched out. She was not handcuffed, but she also had a sack over her head. She was positioned next to George, who looked at her, trying to focus his eyes.

Some of the Triad leaders looked shocked to see a young girl brought before them in this manner. They removed the sack, and Joanne squinted at the bright lights. A scuffle could be heard from the corner of the room.

"Bring out Jason Steed. This is the person who worked undercover and is responsible for many of the deaths of our brothers," Chun Low ordered.

Two men carried Jason out, his hands cuffed behind his back and a sack over his head. Only an hour earlier, he had come around after he had been tranquilized. He wriggled and fought against his two guards. He was dropped on the floor in the center of the hall before the stage. His sack was removed from his head. Immediately the two guards retreated as if they had just released a wild animal.

"Is this a joke? If it is, it's in poor taste. This is a child," an elder deputy leader said, Chun Low looking down the long table at him.

"No, *this* is Jason Steed. It was he who broke into the castle last night," Chun Low replied. Jason's eyes adjusted to the light. He noticed George and Joanne kneeling down on the floor. "What have you to say to us, boy?" Chun Low asked. Jason ignored him. Instead, he made eye contact with Joanne.

"Did they hurt you?" he asked loudly and angrily.

She climbed up and ran to him and put her arms around him. Jason looked at George and gave a slight nod.

"I never thought I would see you again," Jason said and smiled. George gave half a smile and winked at Jason. He was shocked to see the condition of him.

"Ah, young love…how sweet. I asked you a question Steed," Chun Low said.

Jason turned and looked at him and the others seated all around him. He was certain he would soon be killed and would stay defiant to the end.

"So *this* is the big, brave world of the Triads. You capture a schoolgirl and an overweight policeman for doing his job." Jason shook his head as if reprimanding them. "Wow, the mafia has nothing on you guys. You Triads are really hardcore bad guys. If you want me to speak, let her go. If not, go fly a kite."

Outraged, Low nodded at the guards behind Jason. They grabbed Joanne and threw her on the floor. Another guard took out a leather whip and whipped Jason across his back. The crack of the whip cut deep into his skin. He cried out in pain and fell to his knees.

"You will not disrespect us. You will answer the question," Low ordered.

Jason slowly stood. He had tears of pain running down his cheeks. The large room fell silent. Just the sniff from Jason could be heard.

"What do you want to know?" he asked quietly with his head bowed in defeat.

"Boudica. Where is she?"

It then occurred to Jason that they had not found her body yet. He was pleased to have the upper hand. "We had a conversation on her balcony, and we sort of had a falling out. Well, actually, she was the one who fell out," he said and laughed.

"You think this is amusing? We will see how funny you think it is when we take the whip to the girl."

"No, let them go. They are both children. *I* am the SYUI officer that started this. It's me you have the bloody beef with. She's just a little girl who has nothing to do with this. As for Jason, look at the state of him. It was me who got him involved in this. Let them go," George said and stood.

"You almost lost your son. That's a heavy price to pay for someone just doing his job," Low said, stopped, and took a drink of water. He then spoke in a whisper to the others around him. For five minutes, a small hum of whispering could be heard. George was joined by Joanne. Eventually Chun Low stood. The room fell into silence, awaiting his word.

"It is decided. You will be taken from here and executed at first light. We are a wounded organization but will recover. Many men and women have died. The girl stays with us. We need her to bargain with her father."

"What about Jason?" Joanne shouted.

Low looked at the girl and then studied Jason, who was still standing, his hands cuffed behind his back.

"The boy and George Young will be executed."

"No!" a person shouted from the back of the room. He made his way to the front of the stage and walked past Jason and stood in front of Low and the other leaders.

"No, I forbid it. Boudica was my aunt. She was a Dragon leader and a great Triad. He killed her. As part of our oath, I want to kill him the traditional way. It's my right as the nephew of Boudica," he commanded. Some of the high council nodded in agreement. Low looked at the young man and the others on the council.

"Very well. Take off his handcuffs," Low ordered.

Jason watched the young man, who still had his back to him, as he removed his shoes and socks. They took the handcuffs off Jason and stood back. Jason was still not sure what was happening. He looked up at Low and shrugged his shoulders.

"Jason Steed, you have been challenged by a member of Boudica's family. The fight has one rule. To win, you kill the opponent," Low said. Jason noticed a hint of sympathy in his voice. Jason looked at George and Joanne in disbelief. George could not face him, so he looked away.

The young nephew of Boudica removed his jacket and shirt. His muscular back was V-shaped, and he had a slim waist. The triceps in the back of his arms protruded from his soft, young skin. He turned and faced Jason and then smiled.

"Jet Chan," Jason gasped.

CHAPTER 32

Jason Steed, we meet again…for one last time." Jet flexed his muscles and displayed a perfect six pack down his stomach. He raised himself to his toes and started to warm up. Jet Chan was sixteen—four years older than Jason. In Hong Kong, he had trained at a rival karate school. They had crossed swords once and then had met in the Hong Kong's under-sixteen karate championships final. It was a very close, hard-fought fight. Jason had won by one point.

But after the competition, Jason and his father moved to England, and Jet went on to win the world karate under-sixteen championships. Jason hadn't entered, and people in the karate world whispered and wondered who would have won in a rematch.

Slowly Jason removed his shoes and socks. He took off his jacket and shirt, revealing the horrific cuts and bruises on his small body. Since he had left Hong Kong a year ago, Jason had belonged to two karate schools in London, but he had been disappointed with the standard. He was very concerned how he would fair against Jet now. In Hong Kong, Jason had trained under Wong Tong, but recently, Jason's instructors had less knowledge than he had had.

Jason stepped back and closed his eyes, trying to concentrate—trying to remember everything Wong Tong had told him. His heart was beating fast, and he felt nervous as he tried to pump himself up.

Come on. You have beaten him before. You can do it again.

Jet Chan bowed and then Jason did. They stepped back in an attack stance and watched each other. Without warning, Jet ran forward and threw a dummy kick with his left leg and then quickly switched to his right. Jason should have known better, but he was caught by Jet's heel smack in the center of his nose. He was thrown to the ground, and he cried out in pain. A torrent of blood started cascading down Jason's body. His broken nose was painful enough before. Now the severe pain caused his eyes to well up with watery tears, and blood continued to rain down his face. He quickly jumped to his feet to defend himself despite his terrible pain. His eyes continued to stream tears while blood stained his face.

Jet moved with amazing speed. He was in a combat stance one moment and was a blur of movement the next. Jason felt a foot kick him in the chest. The world spun around, and he was thrown to the ground, winded and bruised. Painfully, Jason picked himself up. Jet smiled and nodded. He lashed out again, throwing fast punches at Jason from all angles. Jason blocked punch after punch. He was finding it hard and kept retreating until he had his back up against the stage and could retreat no more.

Jet's advantage of reach and power was proving too much for Jason. It took everything he had to defend himself. A fast, powerful left fist connected with Jason's ribs, and he felt them crack. Jason tried to move away to the left, but his legs were swept away and sent into the air. It was a move that Jason would normally do to his opponents. It humiliated him to be knocked onto his back.

As Jason landed, he rolled away and sprang to his feet. As he turned, he was kicked again. This time, he was caught in the groin. Jason fell again and doubled over in pain. Jet pounced on him, pinned Jason to the ground, and kneeled on Jason's arm. He was now stuck and unable to defend himself and in unbearable pain. Jet unleashed a savage attack of punches directed at Jason's face.

All Jason could do was turn his head away to protect his face. His ear split open, and his neck sustained a torrent of blows. Blood still poured from his nose but now also his mouth. His arms flopped to the ground. It was nearly over for him. Jet was coming in for the kill. Jason saw it in his face.

"Leave him alone. He's hurt," Joanne screamed as she ran up to Jet and pushed him off Jason. Jet jumped to his feet and performed a roundhouse kick, catching her in the face and sending her back where she came from. Jason forced himself up from the ground and again stood to defend himself. He was crouched over, his right arm down by his side, trying to protect his ribs. Jason concentrated, trying to induce an adrenaline rush into his body. He knew he didn't have long left. He grew angry at Jet—angry at himself and Boudica.

George looked away from the fight. He felt helpless and guilty as he watched Jason slowly being beaten to death yet courageously fight on to the end.

Jet attacked again, performing high kicks, trying to catch Jason's face. Jason moved away, still blocking and defending himself. Then out of the corner of his eye, he noticed Joanne. She sat on the floor, holding her face. She was crying and bleeding after Jet's kick. Jet again attacked Jason, but this time, Jason blocked and pushed him off easily. His mind was elsewhere—his body instinctively going through various karate blocks. His body took over as he stepped outside himself. Jet still attacked, jumping from right foot to left foot and throwing everything he had at Jason.

"Don't you know it's wrong to hit girls?" Jason murmured.

Jet paused and stood back, still bouncing back and forth on his toes.

"What?" he asked.

Jason took a good look at Joanne, and he started to shake. In his mind, he could hear Wong Tong telling not to fight in anger, but it was too late. Seeing Joanne crying with blood on her face incensed him. Jason glared at Jet. He rose up on his toes. His pupils dilated and turned black. He walked forward, gritting his teeth. For the first time, Jason attacked. He changed style from tae kwon do to kung fu and then to jujitsu—moves that Jet had not encountered before. Jason moved in close to take away Jet's reach advantage and used his speed to attack Jet.

Jet was now trying to block Jason's punches. Jason used the pain in his body to induce an adrenaline rush. He hit faster and faster. Eventually some got through and connected with Jet's face. He continued on faster and faster. His mind blocked out everything around him. He hopped from one foot to the next. His legs catapulted out with terrific speed and accuracy. Jet was getting hurt and continued to retreat.

Jason threw an avalanche of punches, followed by high kicks. He grunted like an animal as his lungs gasped for oxygen to feed his hungry body. His arms felt like lead, bruised and battered.

His mind tried to block out the pain. Moving quick as lightning, Jason swept Jet's feet away from him, sending him awkwardly to the ground. Jet had been in this position before. Only this time, he twisted and landed on his front. He hoped to get up quickly.

Jason didn't give him the courtesy of a break. He followed Jet down to the floor and swiftly wrapped his right elbow under Jet's neck. Jason's left hand grabbed the side of Jet's head, and he pulled. Jet couldn't move. Apart from the rasping sound of Jason's labored breathing, the entire room fell silent.

All Jason had to do now was twist, and he would break Jet's neck and kill him. Jet knew it. They all knew it. Jet went limp and opened his fists and laid his hands palms down on the ground in surrender. Jason looked around the room. He spoke loudly and directly at Low.

"Too many have died over this. It's over. I have no fight with Jet. My fight was with Boudica, and now she's gone. I will spare his life in return for my own. We have all lost enough. Let it be over." Jason looked up at Low.

Low looked up and down the table at the others. They nodded.

"You are a brave warrior but foolish. I told you the simple rules. To win, you must kill the opponent," Low repeated.

Jason released the grip on Jet's head and neck and forced himself to his feet. Jet spit up blood, and Jason glanced at Joanne, who ran over to help him stand and support his weight.

"Those are your rules, not mine. I was right the first time. You are a bunch of cowards," Jason spat.

He helped Jet to his feet. Jet was embarrassed. He couldn't look Jason in the eye.

"Take them away," Low ordered.

All three were taken by armed guard at gunpoint to a cell deep below the castle. George and Jason were to be executed the following morning. Low would contact Joanne's father and agree to hand her over once he released the Triad's money.

The cell was cold and dark. A small light bulb hung from a wire. Jason found the cell freezing, damp, and smelling of mold and urine. He immediately took in his surroundings. He paced around the cell, looking for a way out, thumping the walls, stamping on the floor, trying to find a hollow sound.

"Jason, son, give it up. It's over. There is no way out of here. I have been in here for two days," George said glumly.

Jason continued to pace up and down.

Joanne walked toward him and caught his arm. "Sorry you got into this, Jason. My people are barbaric," Joanne cried.

Jason stopped and held her. "No, your people are very proud. Your father is a good man. There are just a few bad ones," he said, holding her tight. Eventually he sat down on the floor next to her, defeated.

Jason was not a religious boy. He never really liked going to church and kept his views to himself regarding his faith and what he understood about it. He believed someone was watching over him—maybe his mother, God, or Jesus—but whoever it was, that idea gave him comfort. He closed his eyes and thought of his grandparents and his friends, namely Scott and Catherine. Then he thought of his father and started to quietly cry. Joanne tried to comfort him. It was a pathetic scene. The once-proud and -confident Jason Steed was now broken. George felt ashamed of himself that he had brought the boy into the case. He tried to ignore Jason's whimpers.

A scuffle was heard outside the cell door. The keys were put in the lock, and the door opened. *Are they here to execute us?* Jason wondered. A man walked in and shone a flashlight in Jason's face.

CHAPTER 33

"YOU'D BETTER NOT BE crying. I just risked my life to break you out. At least let me see you're worth it," Jet Chan said, holding out his hand.

"Jet?" Jason asked, wiping his face.

"Come on. We don't have much time. Follow me and keep quiet."

Jason, George, and Joanne followed him to the cell door. Jet stopped and looked at them.

"Not the girl. She stays. Don't worry. She won't be harmed. She is too valuable. Just you two," Jet said, pointing at Jason and George.

"No, she comes with us, Jet. I won't leave without her," Jason said, holding her hand.

"Jason, I've never liked you. I doubt I ever will. You are always so…noble," Jet said and then sighed. "Whatever…just be quick."

Outside the cell, the prison guard was lying on the ground, motionless, with a small amount of blood from his nose. His neck had been broken. They stepped over the body and followed Jet up the many stone stairs to a dark oak door.

"On this other side of this is an armed guard and then freedom. Get as far away as fast as you can, and if you get caught, it was not me who released you," Jet said slowly as he unlocked the door.

The bright light stung their eyes as the aged door creaked

open. Jet went first, followed by George. A startled guard on the other side turned and pointed his gun at Jet. When he saw George following, he approached. Jet sprang into action and attacked the guard, knocking the gun from his hand with a high kick.

"Run!" Jet shouted as he fought with the guard.

George, Jason, and Joanne started to run away from the castle toward the square. A gunshot rang out. Jason turned to see Jet holding his gun, blood oozing from a wound from the fallen guard. As he closed the door, his eyes met Jason's. They both nodded at each other. A single nod, but it meant a lot to both boys.

The alarm sounded. The doors opened, and armed guards swarmed out of the castle. George, Jason, and Joanne had almost made it to the town square. A wedding was taking place at the church. A newlywed couple was walking down the stairs toward an awaiting, shiny, vintage white Rolls-Royce convertible.

A car screeched to a halt, and more guards climbed out and followed on foot. George shouted to onlookers to call the police. A few gunshots rang out, and some of the townsfolk screamed. Jason ran for the Rolls-Royce, tugging Joanne with him. He climbed over the door and opened the driver's side for George.

"George, get in and drive," Jason shouted.

Joanne had been with Jason long enough to read his mind. She had already jumped in behind him. Jason snatched the chauffeur's keys from his hand and threw them to George while the stunned chauffeur protested.

The twelve-cylinder Rolls-Royce engine roared as George put the accelerator pedal to the floorboard. The wheels squealed as they spun and tried to grip the damp surface of the road. The

Rolls-Royce sped off away from the church to the sound of angry protests from the congregation, although they went silent and started running back in the church when they heard gunfire.

The white luxury car sped along, closely followed by three black Mercedes. George crunched his way through the gearbox.

"Faster, George. They're gaining on us!" shouted Jason, who was kneeling on the front passenger seat and looking at his pursuers. The large, wooden-spoked wheels and thin tires on the vintage Rolls-Royce were no match for the modern tires of the Mercedes. They got closer and started shooting. Joanne screamed and lay on the floor between the front and backseats.

As much as George tried, he could not get away. He risked taking a corner too fast and skidded off the road. The Rolls hit a small wall and flipped over. Jason was thrown into the air and landed awkwardly on his right leg, spraining his ankle. George and Joanne stayed with the car as it rolled over twice and ended on its side, now covered in mud.

Jason lay on the damp, snow-covered grass on his back, looking up in pain. Clouds swiftly moved across the sky, which gave him a spectacular view of Mont Blanc. Then something dark and heavy passed over him, and the figure was quickly followed by another. The wind whisked up the light covering of snow all around him.

Two helicopters landed next to Jason. The French police working with MI6 and Interpol were there to storm the castle. An unfamiliar face bent down and pulled Jason to his feet.

"Nice to finally meet you, Jason. Simon Caldwell, SYUI. We spoke on the phone." Caldwell introduced himself.

"You're the guy who wanted me shot," Jason snapped back, giving Caldwell one of his evil looks.

"I was following orders, Jason. Anyway, looks like it turned out okay in the end—what, what?" Caldwell replied in his upper-class accent.

Jason didn't reply. Instead, he looked for Joanne. He limped over to the ambulance, where they were treating her cuts. Simon Caldwell gingerly followed.

"What the dickens are you doing here?" George asked when he saw Caldwell.

"Hello, George. When my top man is involved, I pull out all the stops. It's not just MI6 that can work on international affairs."

"Good, maybe you can get me a job in the Virgin Islands," George joked.

"I need to debrief you and Jason. We have it from the highest authority that the Chinese are sending their top agent to meet Joanne and escort her back to China. You three can accompany me to the airport. It should be safe now, but you can never be too sure," Caldwell ordered.

CHAPTER 34

INTERPOL ARRESTED OVER SEVENTY-NINE Triad members. Most were wanted in various countries. George, Jason, and Joanne were escorted to a van with blackened windows. Simon Caldwell went with them. MI6 agent Gary Barnes drove them to the airport.

Jason sat in the back with Joanne. His ankle was bandaged, and he had a tight bandage around his chest to support his cracked ribs—his cuts cleaned and dressed. They held hands and said nothing—both exhausted by the events of the past week. George sat in front, smoking a cigar someone had given him. Caldwell sat up front with the driver.

George was half asleep and didn't notice anything unusual. Jason sat with his head resting on Joanne's. As the minibus took a very steep turn, George eventually noticed something was wrong.

The lane came to the stop at a ski slope. A helicopter was waiting for them next to a large wooden building with a cable car that went up the mountain.

"What's this? Why have we come here?" George asked.

Jason looked up through his blond bangs.

"We are meeting the Chinese agent. He will take Joanne in the helicopter," Caldwell replied.

Jason went to move. His instincts told him this was wrong. As soon as he tried, Caldwell took out a gun and pointed it at him.

"How did you guess, Jason?" he asked.

"The top Chinese agent was killed outside the police station," Jason said and sat back down.

Caldwell turned the gun on Gary Barnes and fired a single shot, killing the man. His body slumped over the steering wheel, sounding the horn. Caldwell opened the driver's door and pushed Gary's body out onto the ground.

Three men dressed in black emerged from the helicopter and waited.

"You would betray your country for money?" George asked, disgusted.

"You never were the brightest bulb in the box, were you, George? It's not just money. It's power. Once we take over Chairman Mao's weak Chinese government, I shall be given a position in high authority. And I may do even better now that Boudica is gone." He turned to the three men from the helicopter and said, "Take the girl and wait at our warehouse. I will follow, but first, I need to show George and Jason the beautiful mountain scenery."

"No, thanks. I'll stay with Joanne and have a helicopter ride," Jason said and grinned.

"If you want to die a painful death, keep talking. After the trouble you have caused, I would like to see you suffer. George, bring his body," Caldwell said and pointed at Gary Barnes.

George dragged the body behind as he followed Caldwell, who was walking backward toward the cable car building. He never took the gun off Jason.

The building smelled damp and musty. It was dusty and full

of cobwebs because it had been closed for the summer. Once the heavy snowfalls arrived, it would come to life with tourists and skiers. Caldwell turned on the power switches and then a hum of power and lights came on. He pulled down a heavy switch that operated the cable. The cars all started to squeak and slowly move. The cable was a continuous loop.

The cable cars would go up and around a pulley over a mile away and then come back down on a return cable. At the cable building at the bottom, the cars would follow the cable around another pulley and go back up again. The cars never stopped. They could carry about six people. Once you were inside either the top or bottom building, you could simply step on and off the slow-moving cars.

"Get on and take him with you," Caldwell ordered. George pulled the body of Gary Barnes onto a car. Jason jumped on behind, followed by Caldwell with the gun.

As the cable car left the building to make its ascent up the mountain, Jason looked out the window. He could see the men forcing Joanne into the helicopter.

"You will never get away with this," George cursed.

"Sadly, you will never know. Your bodies will be covered by the winter snow that's about to fall. You won't be found until next spring. I assure you I will get away with it," he replied with a smug look on his face.

Jason was infuriated with the way the three men forced Joanne into the helicopter. He stared at Caldwell and concentrated—his eyes darkening. His ears blocked out all sound, and his pupils dilated. Jason's body started to tremble from the adrenaline rush.

Jason slowly raised himself onto his toes. Every muscle fiber in his body tightened like a coiled spring. His heart rate increased, pumping oxygen to his muscles. The fastest human could run a hundred meters in under ten seconds. Caldwell was less than three meters away and was about to get hit by a human cannon-ball. Jason had to risk it. He was certain he could move faster than Caldwell could pull the trigger. His body was trembling like a sprinter on a starting line.

Caldwell could see a blur, but before he could respond, Jason was inches from him. Jason had leapt forward and pounced, his right fist aiming for his target's face. Caldwell moved the gun and fired in Jason's direction. The loud bang exploded in their ears. The bullet passed through Jason's jacket collar, grazed his neck, and went through a window, causing a terrific crash. Jason's fist split open Caldwell's nose. In shock, the man dropped the gun. With his momentum, Jason swung with his left hand at Caldwell again and caught the man directly in the face. Caldwell's legs gave out, and he fell on the floor. Shards of broken glass rained down on him and Jason.

He was pinned down by Jason, who threw punch after punch into Caldwell's face. His hands moved like two powerful pistons pumping away like a finely tuned machine. Jason's attack was vicious, merciless, and unrelenting. George picked up the gun. He knew he wouldn't need it now. Blood started to splatter into Jason's face from Caldwell. The man lay motionless while his face was being broken.

"Jason, stop. Dear God, please stop!" George screamed through broken teeth and bloody lips. "You'll kill him."

Jason stood outside himself and coldly watched what he was doing. There was something horribly methodical about the act as he beat Caldwell's face to a bloody pulp.

"Jason, stop," George shouted.

Jason paused as he was kneeling on Caldwell. He lowered his hands down and fought for his breath.

Joanne.

He looked out the broken window. The helicopter had started up. It would take at least thirty minutes for the cable car to reach the top and come back down again. He looked down and cursed. They were already over one hundred feet above the ground.

George checked Caldwell for a pulse. It was faint, but he was still alive. Jason growled in frustration as the cable car took him higher and farther away from Joanne. Then he noticed it. They were about to pass a car coming down. George watched Jason and could see his plan.

"No, Jason, it's too far," George said. "If you miss, it's certain death! You're still injured. Don't even think about it, son."

Jason ignored him. He had to stop the helicopter from taking off. He took the gun from George and stuffed it down the front of his pants. George shook his head and gave a tight-lipped smile. He knew he couldn't stop him. Jason climbed out of the broken window and stood on the window frame.

"Jason, don't risk it," George begged.

The car came alongside theirs and then Jason leapt from the window, his arms outstretched. Jason managed to get both hands on the brass bar that helped the cars follow around the pulleys, and he held on tightly. His face and body smashed against the side. He screamed out in pain as he knocked his damage nose and ribs. George shook his head in disbelief.

The car seemed to take its time to get back. The helicopter blades spun at high speed. The wind blew the light snow on the ground into a mist. The pilot increased the power slowly, and the helicopter started to lift off the ground.

Jason dropped the last fifteen feet and ran to the helicopter. Next to the building, he noticed a Coca-Cola crate with a few empty bottles inside. He grabbed it and spilled out the bottles as he ran. The helicopter was now off the ground by six feet and going higher. Jason swung the crate up like he was bowling a cricket ball and threw it at the helicopter. The rear rotor blades that controlled the steering smashed the crate into matchsticks.

A loud grinding and crunching noise followed, and the blade sent shards of splinters in all directions. The rotor blades were broken and twisted. The pilot had to land the helicopter before it went into an uncontrollable spin. Jason lay down and took out the gun.

He fired and hit the first man who attempted to climb out. The wounded man fell onto the ground and held his stomach. The other two men stayed inside the relative safety of the helicopter. Jason could see them talking to each other and waving their arms, unsure about what move to make. They did what he dreaded. They put a gun to Joanne's head and made her step out.

What do I do now?

Unsure what to do, he did the exact opposite of what they would have expected. He shot at the helicopter just a few feet from Joanne. She looked horrified.

"Stop! You'll hit the girl," one of the gunmen shouted.

"I don't care. I'm going to kill all of you. Unless you throw out your guns and surrender," Jason shouted back. He shot again, and this time, he came very close to Joanne.

Oops, that was too close.

They paused and then decided that the boy was crazy, so they threw out their guns. They held their hands above their heads. Joanne bent down, picked up the guns, and walked toward Jason. He stood up and gestured for them to come forward.

"You're a good shot, Jase. That was so close to me." Joanne smiled as she hugged him. He never told her he was aiming a lot farther away. They waited for George to come back down in the cable car. He left Caldwell on the car to go around again.

"The fresh air will do him good. Where he's going, he won't get much," George said and grinned.

CHAPTER 35

JASON AND JOANNE WERE taken to a nearby hotel, where they were protected by MI6 and Interpol. George called Joanne's father, Lin Tse-Hsu, who was very pleased to hear his daughter was safe. Joanne spoke to her parents and passed the phone back to George. Jason lay on a bed and smiled at Joanne.

"Was it nice to talk to your parents again?" he asked.

"Yes, Jason, thank you." She sat next to him. They both watched George on the phone.

"Yes, sir, but she will be fine without him," George said. He looked flustered and then turned to Jason. "I can't say. He's not technically my employee. You can ask him, sir." George beckoned Jason to the phone. "Lin Tse-Hsu wishes to speak to you, Jason."

Jason jumped off the bed and took the phone. "Hello, Mr. Lin Tse-Hsu. This is Jason."

"Jason, I wanted to thank you, and if I may, ask one more favor of you," Lin Tse-Hsu said.

"Yes, sir."

"Joanne informs me you have taken care of her, even when the police or MI6 should have been. Although she is being accompanied back to China by MI6, could you come with her just until she is safe with us? If it were not for you, well, I would rather not think about what would have happened."

"Yes, sir, I will. I have never been to China," Jason said and grinned.

"Actually, Jason, I was thinking Hong Kong. I still have some political enemies. I would rather meet in a quiet location in Hong Kong."

Jason beamed. It had been almost two years since he had been in Hong Kong. He missed it and, most of all, his karate instructor, Wong Tong. He arranged to meet at Wong Tong's karate dojo. Jason felt it would be safe.

Two days later, they arrived in Hong Kong via a private Royal Air Force passenger plane. Despite the jet lag and no sleep, Jason was excited about being back in the city he considered home. MI6 drove them to Wong Tong's dojo.

Joanne smiled when she saw Jason's excitement as they were driven through the streets of Hong Kong.

"Look. That's my old school." He pointed at a large white building with a high fence that keep footballs from coming over. "That's the baker shop where we used to buy carrot cake."

She smiled at him and nodded, trying to look interested in everything he pointed out. She had never seen him smile so much.

"There, next to the church, that's Wong Tong's!" he shouted to the driver.

The MI6 officers climbed out and checked to see if the area was clear. They held their jackets down, concealing weapons. One of Lin Tse-Hsu's bodyguards was standing outside. They spoke and nodded. Jason and Joanne climbed out and walked inside, hand in hand.

When Joanne saw her mother, she ran across the floor to meet her and then hugged her parents. Joanne and her mother cried as they hugged. Jason took off his shoes and socks and bowed as he entered.

"Jason Steed," a boy called out. Jason looked up and nodded at him. The students surrounded Jason. Most of them knew him and those who didn't had heard all about Wong Tong's star pupil. Jason shook hands and remarked how many of them had grown. Then he noticed Wong Tong standing quietly in the corner. The students stood back. Jason ran to Wong Tong and stopped just short of hugging him. He bowed and gave his hand. Although he wanted to embrace his mentor, Jason resisted hugging Wong Tong.

"You move back to Hong Kong?" Wong Tong asked in his broken English.

Jason's face saddened. "No, it's just a quick visit."

"You forgot how to block? Is your nose broken?"

"I was head-butted. Yeah, it's broken."

"You were head-butted. You're so small. Was it a midget?" Wong Tong teased.

"Don't laugh. It was a woman."

"Ha, a woman. Jason, you need practice more." Wong Tong laughed. He noticed Lin Tse-Hse approaching.

"Jason, may I thank you?" Lin Tse-Hsu interrupted, holding his hand out. Jason shook his hand and smiled. "We are leaving now," the man continued. "We owe you a great debt, Jason. You must come to China one day as my guest."

"Thank you, sir. I will." He watched them slowly leave, Joanne holding her mother's hand. She couldn't face saying good-bye to Jason. He slowly followed her outside and watched her climb into the back of a black limousine. She looked up and saw him looking at her. She climbed out of the car and ran up to him, crying.

"Jason," she sobbed. He held her tight as her parents watched the two of them. He lifted her chin with his finger and kissed her gently on the lips. Her father was taken by surprise. A Western boy kissing his daughter on the lips in a public place was not appropriate. He walked over to break them up, but when he saw tears running down the boy's face, he stood back and left them alone to say good-bye.

"I'll always love you, Jason." They both smiled as they wiped each other's tears away. It tore at Jason's heart when he watched the car leave. He questioned how he felt about her. It was different than the way he felt about Catherine. He figured it was the same love as a brother and sister would have. Either way, this good-bye hurt, knowing that he may not ever see her again.

As the car drove off, an MI6 officer approached Jason and passed him a tissue to wipe his face. "We have to get a hotel room, son. Our flight to Britain leaves in the morning," he said.

Jason looked up at him, wiped his eyes, and cleared his throat.

"I want to stay here for the rest of the day. Can you pick me up tonight?" Jason asked.

"We're supposed to stay with you, Jason. Mr. Young insisted."

"George should know by now that I never do as I'm told," Jason said as he walked back into the dojo.

Once the lesson was over, Wong Tong and Jason spent a few hours talking.

"So, Jason, in England, do you eat these 'farmer burgers'?" Wong Tong asked.

"Farmer burgers? I don't know what they are."

"Yes, maybe I have the name wrong. I remember the name from the song," Wong Tong explained.

"What song?" Jason asked.

"You know, the 'E, I, E, I, O' song."

"E, I, E, I, O" song?

Jason started to roar with laughter. He tried to speak but was laughing, much to the annoyance of Wong Tong. He held his chest because laughing still hurt his ribs.

"You mean the 'Old MacDonald had a farm' song. You mean McDonald's burgers," he said, laughing. "Yes, I have had them. They're good."

CHAPTER 36

Ray Steed paced up and down the airport lounge, waiting for his son's plane to land. The Boeing 707 rumbled into its gate. Ray watched the passengers walking down the steps, holding small bags and newspapers.

He breathed a sigh of relief and smiled with tears in his eyes when he saw his son. Jason walked along the tarmac toward the terminal, his blond hair blowing across his face in the autumn wind. He looked tiny compared to the two MI6 officers surrounding him.

As Jason emerged in the airport lobby, he noticed his father. Tears ran down his smiling cheeks. Jason ran at his father with his arms open, and Ray kneeled down to catch him. Ray was almost knocked over by his son as Jason collapsed into his father's arms. For a few moments, they said nothing. Jason finally relaxed and felt safe at last. Ray kissed Jason's forehead and face. He inhaled deeply, smelling his son's neck. He ignored everyone around him and cherished his son's scent and touch.

"I was so worried, Jason. Please don't do anything like this again. I don't know what I would do if something happened to you."

"Sorry, Dad. I know you said don't get involved but—"

Ray put his finger up against his son's lips. He lovingly pressed his nose against Jason's forehead. "What's done is done. The main thing is you are home." He kissed him again and looked up at two MI6 officers who were standing over them. Ray stood and picked up Jason, who still had his arms around his father, and shook their hands.

"Thank you. He will be safe now." Ray carried Jason to the parking garage. Jason snuggled his nose into his father neck. He enjoyed feeling like a small boy again. Once in the car, Ray turned and looked at Jason. Jason was surprised to see that his father had tears in his eyes. Ray was just over six feet tall and rarely showed emotion. Jason had never seen his father shed a tear before.

"What's wrong, Dad?" he asked, taking his father's hand.

"I thought I was going to lose you.

"It's fine, Dad. I can look after myself."

"I'm not, Jase. Oh, I know you're a tough little trooper and you always seem to bounce back, but I can't go through that again. Please don't put me through that ever again."

Jason leaned forward and kissed his father. He wiped his father's face and gave a smile.

◉

Scott went directly to the Steeds' house from school. The boys were playing chess in Jason's room, with his cassette player at high volume playing Paul McCartney's latest album, *Band on the Run*.

"I brought Scott's overnight bag," said Dr. Turner, who was dropping Scott off. "I can take a look at Jason now. As soon as he is better, I'd like to get him in for surgery. Broken nose, you say?" Dr. Turner asked as he shook Ray's hand.

"Yes, go on up. Just follow the sound of the music," Ray said.

"I wouldn't call it music, but it's been so quiet here these past few months without him, it's great to hear all the noise again," interrupted Mrs. Beeton. "I'll bring you up a tray of tea."

Dr. Turner made Jason lay on his back while he examined his nose.

"Ouch," Jason said, trying to pull away.

"Yes, sorry, Jason. I want to feel what damage is done." The doctor gently felt the boy's nose and moved it slightly from side to side. "Is this all…this time? No bullet wounds? What happened to your arm? Were you attacked by a lion?"

"It was a leopard," Jason squealed, trying to pull away from the doctor's fingers.

"It's a clean break. It will be a simple fix. You have a healthy body, Jason. Try to take better care of it. I'm sure these scratches and cuts will heal without scars. How did you do it?"

"I told you. A leopard," Jason said, sitting back up. Dr. Turner didn't know if he should believe him or not, but where Jason was concerned, anything could be true.

A letter soon arrived for Jason from China:

Dear Jason,

Saying "thank you" hardly seems sufficient to express my gratitude. But if these words can reflect what is buried deep within my heart, you will know how much I appreciate you and all that you've given.

I know I could never take the place of your girlfriend just like no one can take your place in my life. You will always live in my heart like another soul inside of me.

As long as I draw breath, I will always love you.

Joanne XXX

He never wrote back. He kept the letter and hid it under his bed, where he kept his secret items, which included a pass code to get into SYUI offices, private phone numbers of the royal family, his pilot's license, and a large pocketknife.

Over the next few weeks, normality came back to Jason's life. It was a shock: one day, he was being chased across Europe by gangsters and police, and the next, he was getting told off at school for running down a corridor. Did he miss it? The danger and excitement? "No" was the answer he gave everyone—except Scott. Together, they shared the same desire for adventure.

Jason knew his life would never be the same again. British intelligence now had an ace up its sleeve, and Jason had to overcome his fears and deal with the secret world he was now a part of. He would have to grow a tough shell around himself. Despite his many friends, his grandparents, and the love of his father, he was painfully aware he was very much alone in this world. When it came down to it, there was only one person he could rely on in the world, and he was called Jason Steed.

SCOTT TURNER'S GUIDE TO ENGLISH COCKNEY RHYMING SLANG

Hiya. You may have noticed that smelly George Young speaks weirdly. I'm from North London, so I speak normal. George is from East London, where they talk in slang. "Cockney rhyming slang" is bloody difficult to understand but kinda neat once you get the hang of it. Here's a guide to help you understand what he is talking about:

APPLES AND PEARS, Stairs

BLOODY OR BLEEDING, Curse words used by most British; deemed inoffensive

BROWN BREAD, Dead

BUTCHER'S HOOK, Look. Would be used when someone says, "Take a butcher's at this."

DOG AND BONE, Telephone

JAM JAR, Car

OLD BILL, Police

STITCH THAT, Said at the moment of physical attack, meaning you're going to require stitches after the injury I'm about to inflict on you.

TROUBLE AND STRIFE, Wife

TWO AND EIGHT, State. Would be used when someone says, "You are in a right two and eight," meaning you are in a right state, mess, trouble.

WHISTLE AND FLUTE, Suit. Some Londoners will just say, "I will be wearing a 'whistle.'"